MAGENTA MINE

INVERTARY BOOK 3

JANET ELIZABETH HENDERSON

ISBN: 978-0-473-46131-7

Cover design by Janet Elizabeth Henderson

Editing by Liz Dempsey

❀ Created with Vellum

Harry Boyle fell in love with Magenta when he was eight years old. It happened in the sandpit of the local primary school. The five-year-old girl had been building the biggest sandcastle Harry had ever seen. He'd paused beside her, wondering if he should give her tips on how to make it more structurally sound, but he'd learned the hard way to keep his super brain to himself.

"Hairy Boil," one of the class bullies shouted behind him. "You going to play with the wee girls now?"

There was laughter.

Magenta looked up at him with huge golden eyes, her honey-coloured pigtails askew and full of sand. She blinked several times as she studied him. "That's a funny name. You don't look hairy."

Harry took her comment seriously, as he did most things. "They're making fun of my name. It's Harry Boyle."

She scowled. "That's mean." She studied him a bit more before nodding to herself. "Do you want me to punch them for you?"

Harry's mouth fell open at her words. He looked over his

shoulder at the group of boys who were still pointing at him and laughing, then he looked back at the fairy in the sandpit. He would have laughed too if she hadn't been so serious. The bullying had gotten worse since his brother Flynn had gone to secondary school, and as much as he would like someone to stand up for him, he didn't think a five-year-old girl was the best protector to pick.

"They'll get fed up soon and annoy someone else," he said.

"I don't mind hitting them." She shrugged and turned back to her castle.

Harry couldn't take it anymore. "You need to reinforce it, or it will collapse."

She eyed him thoughtfully. "How?"

Harry sank to his knees beside her and showed her how to make the castle stable.

And that's how his friendship with Magenta started. Of course, back then she was still called Maggie Fraser. It wasn't until she was thirteen, and Harry was in university, that she dyed her hair black, bought a giant tub of eyeliner and started calling herself Magenta. Harry had come back to Invertary for the holidays to find his friend replaced by a sullen Goth who'd looked him up and down slowly, smirked and turned away from him. She'd never turned back.

And Harry had never stopped loving her.

"*She's* the reason you're making us pack up and relocate to the middle of nowhere?" Rachel didn't make any effort to hide her disgust as she pointed at the lingerie shop. Magenta could be clearly seen through the shop window.

Harry looked at his business manager. He'd met Rachel in the university cafeteria when he was sixteen. His big brain had meant that he was years younger than his fellow students and socially out of his depth. Rachel had felt sorry for him and had pretty much adopted him as her pet—at least, that's what it had always felt like to Harry. She'd been older and wiser at nineteen, not to mention she was studying the much more socially savvy business studies course. The friendship had stuck, and eight years later, Rachel was the face of Harry's programming business. And he was grateful for it.

"Her name is Magenta, and she's not the only reason we're moving to Invertary." He glanced around his home-town, with its rows of quirky white and grey crooked houses and cobblestone roads. Heather-covered hills cradled the town, while the cool loch sparkled beside it. "Look around, Rach—this is much nicer than London."

She stuck her tiny nose in the air and folded her arms over her designer blue business suit. Everything about Rachel was polished and expensive. She'd once told him her shoes cost more than his car. Every time he looked at them, he wondered why.

"You know how I feel about this," she said. "It might be pretty up here in the Highlands, but our business contacts are in London and Europe."

"We can conference call. Skype. Fly in for face to face. I don't see the problem. This isn't Outer Mongolia. It's Scotland."

"You can't network over the phone. You do that face to face, over lunch or a casual drink after work. None of which we can do here."

"I don't do that stuff anyway," Harry pointed out.

"No, but I do." She flicked her manicured fingers in the direction of the town. "What am I supposed to do here while you're communing with your laptop? This town is stuck in the fifties. It doesn't even have a decent clothes shop. And you want to drag everyone up here. The team will go insane inside of a week."

"No they won't." Harry sighed. "As long as they have internet access, they won't care. It's only you who'll miss the

London scene. I told you. You can stay there. We'll work it out."

"Who will you bounce ideas off if I'm not here?"

"I can call."

"It won't be the same." She patted the tight bun that held her auburn hair.

He couldn't argue with that. For eight years she'd been his sounding board, and he wasn't sure how he'd function without her. Rachel let out a dramatic sigh.

"Why this girl? I don't see anything special about her. I mean, she works in a lingerie shop and she obviously has no idea how to dress. She didn't even finish school. How are you supposed to have a conversation with her?"

Harry shook his head. Rachel's issues were for Rachel to deal with.

He cocked his head at the shop behind them. Eye Spy was a security company run by ex-SAS member Lake Benson. It was no secret that Harry specialised in security programming, and Lake thought there might be some benefits in a working relationship. So far their meetings had gone well.

"You go in," he told Rachel. "Tell Lake I'll be in in a minute. I'm going to talk to Magenta."

"Fine. I hope it goes better than the last three times you've tried."

"Couldn't be worse," Harry mumbled as he walked over the street to Kirsty's lingerie shop.

"HERE HE COMES AGAIN," Kirsty said from her spot at the window. The ex-model turned to Magenta, who was unpacking a new line in thongs at the back of the shop. "How about this time you let him talk to you instead of doing your best to scare him off?"

Magenta rolled her eyes. "I don't want to talk to him. Just

because we were friends when we were kids, doesn't mean I owe him anything now."

"That's harsh. Even you can be more polite than that. I've seen it. I know it can happen."

"I'm busy," Magenta said. "Tell him to come back later."

"You tell him. I can't. It's like kicking a puppy."

Only if the puppy was over six feet tall, muscled in a lean way and had sexy silver eyes. Magenta clamped down on her thoughts. So Harry had grown up pretty. So what? She still didn't want to deal with him. She heard the bell over the door and felt her body tense. Why the heck didn't he go back to London, where he belonged?

"Hi, Magenta." His deep voice seemed to rumble and vibrate throughout her body.

Taking a steadying breath, she turned towards him. "What can I do for you, Harry?"

She kept her face expressionless, and was grateful that she'd opted for her thigh-high platform boots this morning. She needed the extra height to stop from gazing up at him.

"I thought we could get together tonight. Eat. Talk about old times." He wore a grey T-shirt with Einstein's head on it, and Magenta wondered if Einstein would be proud that he adorned T-shirts and bobblehead dolls.

"Sorry, Harry, I'm busy." She took a step back towards the box of thongs she'd been unpacking.

Out of the corner of her eye she could see Kirsty scowling as she wagged a finger. Magenta ignored her.

"Tomorrow, then." He thrust his hands into the pockets of his faded blue jeans. Magenta knew he was worth a lot of money. It'd been the talk of the town that Harry had sold a program he'd developed to the UK government for millions. It almost made her smile to see he was still wearing his old, tatty jeans. Clothes were never something Harry had noticed as a kid. Not like the designer-clad sidekick he'd dragged to town with him. Everything about her screamed money and class. Magenta frowned at yet another reminder that she would never travel in the same circles as Harry.

"I'm busy for the foreseeable future," she told him.

"Is there a way you can get un-busy?" His smile almost made her crumble. He somehow managed to pull off sexy and sweet at the same time.

"Harry," she said on a sigh. "I don't want to get together and rehash our childhood. I don't want to get together full stop. I know this isn't what you want to hear, but you just need to suck it up."

Any other man would have tucked tail and run at such a blunt rejection. Not Harry. Bloody stupid man. Harry smiled and took a step towards her.

"Well, I would suck it up, if I believed you. But I don't. So how about you clear some time in your busy schedule for me?"

"Not going to happen." She swallowed hard and thrust a handful of pink underwear at him. "You might as well make yourself useful while you annoy me. Sort these into sizes."

Harry looked down at the silky thongs then gave her a wicked smile. "See, this is why we need to spend time getting to know each other again." He moved forwards, crowding her space. "You think handing me lingerie is going to make me turn red, stutter and run. But I keep telling you. I've grown up. I'm not the kid you knew." He took another step towards her, making her breath hitch and her body vibrate at his nearness. "Lingerie doesn't scare me, Magenta. Neither do you." His voice was a low, sexy rumble that woke up her erogenous zones. "I like lingerie." He held up a thong. "These would look good on you."

Magenta sucked in a breath. "Time for you to go, Harry." She was pleased that her voice sounded as sharp as usual.

He placed the underwear on the counter beside her. "I'm not giving up. You and I have unfinished business."

With that, he turned and sauntered out of the shop. Magenta let out a long, slow breath.

"What is wrong with you?" Kirsty flicked her russet-coloured hair out of her eyes before glaring at Magenta. Kirsty had cut it after her accident years ago, but now she was letting it grow out. "You two used to be inseparable. Now you won't even talk to the guy."

"That was a long time ago. People change." Magenta turned her focus back to the underwear as she quietly worked at getting her body back under control.

"Yep, they do. And Harry has changed for the better. You may as well give in and meet with him. See what he wants. You might actually enjoy hanging out with him again."

"Yeah, right. And pigs might fly over Invertary dropping free bacon on everyone."

Magenta turned her back on her boss and concentrated on her work. She didn't know why Harry was so interested in spending time with her. She'd made sure to burn the bridges between them when she was thirteen. It had ripped her apart, but she'd known that it was the right thing to do. For both their sakes.

"How did it go?" Lake asked as Harry let himself into the security shop.

Harry used his hand to mime a plane flying, crashing and exploding.

"That good, huh?" Lake's mouth twitched as it tried to smile.

"Isn't it time you gave up?" Rachel said. "It's obvious she isn't interested in you."

They were sitting at a round conference table in Lake's

back room. Harry pulled out a chair, flipped it, straddled it and leaned on the backrest. "She's interested. When I bumped into her sister a few months ago, she told me Magenta used to write our names together in hearts all over her books. She said Magenta still keeps a scrapbook about me. She's interested, all right. She's just scared."

There was cackling from the corner. "Not a lot scares that lassie," Betty said.

Harry grinned at the eighty-seven-year-old. Betty had always fascinated him. She was known for her lies, her sick sense of humour and her willingness to meddle for entertainment's sake—and she didn't give a damn who knew it. Lake had inherited Betty when he'd bought her shop, and seemed to treat her like some sort of mascot. She was currently installed in her tatty old armchair, feet on a stool, reading a magazine. Harry cocked his eye at the magazine title—*Survivalist Now*. He gave Lake a questioning look.

Lake's lip twitched. "She saw that movie with Will Smith, the one where zombies take over the world. Now she's preparing for a zombie apocalypse."

"Aye, you laugh now, son, but you'll tell a different story when they're out to eat your brains, and the only thing between you and being somebody's snack is the preparation I put in."

Harry stifled a grin as Betty turned her attention back to him. "You need to stop trying to talk to that girl in the shop. You need to get her alone somewhere. A lingerie shop is no place for a heavy discussion."

"Getting her alone is hard. She's either at the shop or in the house she shares with the twins." He shuddered. Dealing with his twin cousins was worse than dealing with the UK government. "Plus, I asked her out to dinner tonight and she turned me down flat."

Betty shifted in her chair, then tugged her hairnet down

over her mostly bald head. "That's where you're going wrong. You don't ask her to go out with you. You surprise her when she's alone, preferably in a place where she can't run away."

"Please tell me you aren't taking relationship advice from Lake's Hobbit," Rachel said.

"Hey," Betty snapped. "Lake's the only one allowed to call me that."

Rachel rolled her eyes dramatically. "Can we please go back to London, where we belong?"

"Aye." Betty gave Rachel the evil eye. "Send her back. She's too stuck up to fit in here."

"So," Harry said loudly to ward off a counterattack from his business manager. "Got any suggestions on how to get her alone?"

"Well, it just so happens that I do." The look on Betty's face was pure mischief. She was clearly up to something, but Harry was too desperate to let it worry him. "Saturday afternoon, Magenta is going into the old mine to take some pictures. She'll be alone. I reckon you should make a picnic and surprise her there."

Huh. That wasn't a bad plan. He looked at Lake, who shrugged. "I wouldn't take relationship advice from Betty either," he said, making Betty grin with pride.

"That's my boy," she told him.

"So where in the mine is she taking photos?" Harry asked.

Betty gave him a toothless grin. "I can't rightly explain it. Best if you pick me up on Saturday and I'll show you the way. There are a lot of mine entrances; it'd be easy for you to go to the wrong one."

"It's a deal," he told her.

"Idiot," Rachel said.

Lake just grinned.

CHAPTER 2

After Harry's visit, Magenta's day really took a nosedive. Every time Kirsty was anywhere near her, she nagged her to spend time with Harry. It had gotten to the stage where Magenta was planning to lock her boss in the storeroom in order to get some peace.

Then, just when she'd managed to get Kirsty to leave the topic alone, the door opened and in walked Harry's designer sidekick—Executive Barbie. As usual, she was scowling. Magenta didn't need Harry's genius IQ to see that the woman didn't want to be stuck in Scotland. With a fortifying breath, she plastered on her fake smile and faced the woman.

"Can I help you with something?" *Please say no. Please say no.* She wasn't in the mood to deal with yet another person's issues.

"I'm Harry's executive manager of operations, Rachel." She said the title as though she was announcing her royal heritage. Magenta kept her face carefully blank. Didn't Harry have less than ten employees? Bet that made "executive managing" a whole lot easier.

"Magenta," Magenta said, because it seemed rude not to give her name.

"I know who you are." Rachel folded her arms over her designer business suit and tapped perfectly manicured nails.

The woman was wearing five-inch stilettos. No wonder she was grumpy. Magenta would be grumpy too if her feet were killing her all day long.

"What can I do for you?" she asked, hoping it would speed things along.

Out of the corner of her eye she could see Kirsty paying close attention to the conversation.

"What can you do?" Rachel gave a mirthless laugh. "You could stay away from Harry. That would be great. You could tell him plainly that you have no interest in him—which you clearly don't—and send him back to London. Where he belongs. Where we both belong."

Magenta clenched her fists. She did not like being told what to do. By anyone.

"I'm not keeping Harry here. Go back to London any time you like."

"Oh, but you are." Rachel pursed her lips in disgust. "He came here to talk to you. Unless you shut that down, he'll stay here until it happens. He can be very stubborn."

"Ha! Pigheaded, more like."

Rachel stared at Magenta. "I want to go back to London. I don't want to move the business up here. The only decent thing about this town is this lingerie shop."

"Thank you," Kirsty shouted from the back of the shop.

Magenta almost rolled her eyes.

"The people we need to deal with are in London. Not this backwater. This cultural desert. This haven for inbred—"

Magenta held up a hand. "I get it. Invertary bad. London good."

Rachel frowned, then forced a smile. "We both know you

aren't interested in Harry. Whatever you two were to each other is in the past. And I think you'd like to keep it there. So why don't you make that clear to him and we'll all be happy?" She turned towards the door. "Think about it," she ordered.

The door closed loudly behind her. Kirsty came up to stand beside Magenta. They stared at the door.

"I know who she reminds me of," Kirsty said. "Remember in one of the X-Men movies there was a woman with an adamantine skeleton, like Wolverine? They fought. Wolverine won. Wolverine will always win, because he's the perfect man." Kirsty gave a wistful sigh as she pointed at Rachel's back. "That's who she is. She's the evil version of Wolverine."

Magenta stared at her friend for a moment. "Does your fiancé know about this unhealthy obsession you have with a superhero?"

Kirsty smiled. "You're not going to do what she told you to, are you? She warned you off. Isn't that like your version of a red flag to a bull? Shouldn't you charge out there to spend time with Harry purely to defy her ultimatum?"

"Contrary to popular belief, I am an adult. I'm not going to do something I don't want to do in order to spite a crazy stranger. She's Harry's problem. I don't want anything to do with either of them."

"She is right about one thing," Kirsty said. "Harry is very stubborn. If he wants to spend time with you, he'll make it happen."

"He can try." Magenta stormed back to the rack she was cleaning.

"What is your problem, anyway? Why are you so set against Harry? You two used to be close. What did he do that's so unforgivable?"

Magenta felt her stomach clench. "It wasn't him. It was me. I said things that were unforgivable."

"Harry seems to have gotten over it."

"Maybe, but the reasons I said those things haven't changed. Harry is better off far away from me. And I'm sure I'm better off without him in my life. If we try to reboot our friendship, we'll only get hurt. It's smarter to stop it before it starts."

Kirsty eyed her keenly. "He hurt you."

"No." Magenta turned away from her friend. "But he could have. I stopped it before it got that far."

She felt Kirsty's hand on her shoulder, her touch gentle. "You loved him."

Magenta stopped breathing. Kirsty Campbell was far too perceptive for her own good.

"Of course I loved him," Magenta scoffed. "We were best friends."

"No." Kirsty shook her head. "You were *in* love with him."

For a minute the pain of the past overwhelmed Magenta. She closed her eyes and reminded herself to breathe. When she opened them, she shook Kirsty's hand off.

"A stupid teenage crush. I grew up. I got over it. It's time Harry got over the past too." With that, she walked away from Kirsty. She was done talking about Harry.

AFTER A LONG DAY AT WORK, Magenta entered the flat she shared with her twin best friends to find the phone ringing.

"Don't answer it," she shouted, but it was too late. She could already hear Claire tell Magenta's mother that she'd just come through the door. Great. The icing on the cake of death that was her day. She slipped off her boots, dropping in height by several inches, before holding out her hand for the phone.

"Sorry," Claire, one half of her twin roommates, whispered as she handed it to Magenta.

Magenta pursed her lips. They paid extra for caller ID so that they would know who was calling before picking up. They paid extra so that Magenta could avoid her mother. Right now it was money wasted. She took a deep breath as Claire tiptoed away. Why she was tiptoeing was anyone's guess.

"Mum." Magenta felt her stomach tighten as the word came out of her mouth.

"Maggie, honey, I wouldn't bother you, but I need a wee favour." Her mother's soft whine made Magenta cringe. As did being called Maggie.

"What do you want, Mum?" Magenta had to work hard to stop from biting out the words. Since leaving home when she was sixteen, her mother had called at least twice a day to "not bother" Magenta.

"I wouldn't ask, but…" Her voice faded to a pathetic nothingness.

"What is it?" Magenta squeezed the words through clenched teeth.

"Mr Morrison put a note through my door about the hedge. He's complaining about my side of it again. I don't have the strength to deal with the hedge. It's so much work trimming it. I've been meaning to find a teenager to come cut it for me, but I haven't been well enough to get to it yet. I wondered if you would have a word with him."

Magenta closed her eyes and tried to think of something calming. Anything calming. It didn't work. Her mind was blank. Mainly she wanted to kick old man Morrison's backside for leaving a note instead of waiting until her mother was home and dealing with her in person.

"Mum, he's your neighbour. He's right next door. I'm on the other side of town. I think you should talk to him."

"Oh, no, I can't do that. You know how he gets. It would be best if you came over and dealt with it. You know I wouldn't impose if I was feeling better." She took a deep, shaky breath. "I've been feeling so faint this past week. I nearly passed out in the supermarket. Lorraine Buchanan had to fetch me a chair from the staff room. They made me a cup of tea, and Lorraine sat patting my hand until the dizzy spell passed. She's such a lovely girl. I told her all about you taking care of me."

Magenta almost choked on the words she wanted to say. There was nothing wrong with her mother. The woman made almost daily trips to the doctor and they'd never found anything wrong with her. Ever since their father had left when Magenta was nine, her mother had been "ill." Sometimes it was hard to remember that the woman was barely fifty.

"Why don't you phone Mr. Morrison? If you're too weak to walk next door, you can make a call. You had enough energy to call me."

There was a long sigh. "Aye, you're right, sweetheart. I could probably call, but this has taken a lot out of me and I'll need to lie down when I hang up." She made that pathetic little mewing noise that made Magenta cringe.

"If you had enough energy to make one call, why did you make it to me instead of to your neighbour?"

She knew the answer already—she couldn't make Mr. Morrison dance like a puppet on a string, but with a few master manipulations she could manage it with her daughter.

Her mother let out a little moan. The kind people make when feeling weak. The kind she'd spent years perfecting. "You are so much better at dealing with conflict than I am." That whining voice went right through Magenta. "You've always been so good at standing up for yourself. Ever since you were a wee lassie and the kids in school made fun of you because you weren't as smart as they were. I feel terrible that

I was never well enough to help you with that, but you dealt with it great on your own. You may not be as clever as other folk, but you're so good at dealing with people. I don't know what I'd do without you."

It was amazing how her mother could slice into her self-esteem at the same time as praising her. Magenta rubbed her temple to ward off the headache that was creeping up on her. Immediately she snapped up straight. She was doing it. She was manufacturing symptoms. She was turning into her mother. She let her hand drop to her lap.

"Fine," Magenta said through clenched teeth. "I'll come talk to the neighbour."

"You're a good girl. I don't know what I'd do without you. You're nothing like Grace; she doesn't spare a thought for her mother. So selfish. But I can always rely on you. Your older sister may have the brains in the family, but you have other gifts."

As usual, she never mentioned what those other gifts might be.

"I need to go," Magenta said. "I'll be over later."

"Use your key. I'll probably be lying down."

Like that was something new. "Sure."

"Love you, sweetie," her mother said.

Magenta mumbled something and hung up. If her mother loved her, then she sure as hell didn't like the way love felt. It was a nasty emotion. Like slime oozing through her veins.

"Sorry," Claire said from the stove, where she was cooking dinner. "I didn't think before I answered the phone."

"Never mind," Magenta told her. It wasn't her friend's fault that her mother drove her mad.

"I printed out those forms for you." Claire used her wooden spoon to point to the papers on the tiny dining table. "You keep putting it off, but we both know you'd love to become a caving instructor. It's time to get on with it and get that qualification."

Magenta forced a smile as she reached for the paperwork. "You know me. Procrastination is my middle name."

"That's why you need friends like us."

"I'll take these to my room and I'll fill them out after I deal with my mum."

"Don't forget. I'll be checking. You've been dreaming about running a caving business for years. It's time you turned that dream into reality. If you don't get your bum in gear you'll be working for Kirsty until you're ninety."

Magenta faked a laugh as she headed to her room at the front of the house. Once inside, she shut the door and leaned against it. She looked at the forms in her hand. The words jumped and wobbled, as they usually did. She smothered a frustrated scream. She didn't need to be able to read the form to know the requirement. Her caving mentors had told her about the written exam.

After one last look at the paperwork, she ripped it into tiny pieces before putting it in the bin. She should never have mentioned her dream to the twins, because that's just what it was—a dream. It would never be reality. Not for her. Not for a woman who was too stupid to even finish school. A woman who struggled to read a simple form. No. She wiped her eyes and sniffed. Dreams were for other people.

With a heavy sigh, she changed into jeans and boots before heading off to deal with her mother.

CHAPTER 3

Harry should never have listened to Betty. She was evil incarnate. Entertaining evil. But evil nonetheless. His big brain had failed him. Betty had hacked his IQ and uploaded a virus. A virus called hope.

Which was how he'd found himself trapped in an abandoned mine outside of Invertary, waiting to be rescued and praying that the hill wouldn't collapse on his head.

"You're a bloody idiot, you know that?" his cousin Matt Donaldson, the sole police presence in Invertary, shouted through the air vent next to the door. The door that Betty had jammed shut.

Yes. He was that much of an idiot. He'd been trapped in a mine by a tartan-clad geriatric. It didn't get much more stupid than that.

"Are you there, moron?" Matt's voice echoed through the cavernous room where Harry was currently trapped.

"Where else would I be, dumbass?" Harry called back.

He heard laughter. No doubt Matt had already texted Harry's older brother Flynn to fill him in. Growing up in the shadow of "the testosterone twins" had been no easy task for a certified geek. The fact the three boys had managed to stay close friends was a miracle. But then, they'd had to unite at an early age to defend themselves against Matt's younger twin sisters.

"Flynn says I've to take pictures," Matt said.

Harry hung his head. Yep. He wasn't going to live this down anytime soon.

"Seriously," Matt said. "You okay in there? Don't go wandering off. Stay near the door so we know where you are."

Harry surveyed his surroundings, which were dim in the faint sliver of light that seeped in from around the door. Without his flashlight on, he could make out shadows and shapes for a couple of feet in front of him, then it all turned to inky blackness. At least it wasn't damp. He sat on the floor, leaning against the wall beside the door, his legs stretched out in front of him. According to the clock on his phone, he'd been in the mine about an hour. It felt longer.

"I'm fine. I'm great. I'm waiting on a megaton of rock and dirt to fall on my head and crush my brain like a grape, but apart from that I'm hunky-dory. When are you going to get me out of here?"

At least Betty had called for help after she'd locked him in.

"Hunky-dory? Is that what all the cool kids are saying these days?" Matt was laughing at him. Seven years older than Harry, his cousin found every opportunity he could to call him a kid.

Harry worked to stop grinding his teeth to dust. "When this kid gets out of here, he's going to kick your backside for taking the piss."

There was laughter. "You might be good at that fancy martial arts stuff, Harry boy, but I can still take you in a fight."

Yeah. Right. "What's happening? What are you doing to get me out of here?"

"Well, here's the thing." Matt sounded like he was grinning. "The door is seriously warped. There's a warning sign on it so that no one will shut it. Its spring-loaded, and about ten inches thick. Every time it slams shut, it shakes things loose above it. We need to make sure it's possible to open it without causing the entrance to weaken. Last time this happened, it took two days to get it open."

Harry shot to his feet. "Two days?"

"Don't tell me you're scared," Matt mocked.

Harry's super brain calculated the chances of a cave-in. He didn't like the odds he came up with. The mine was over 150 years old. When was the last time there was a collapse? He needed more data. He reached for his phone, ready to do an internet search, but remembered he had no connection.

"I need more data. When was the last time this mine collapsed?" He tried to keep the worry out of his voice.

"Not since I've been the police in town."

That was what? Seven years. That wasn't long. Harry wasn't reassured. He was going to die trapped underground. It was not the way he thought he would go. He assumed he'd die of unrequited love.

Matt's voice cut through his anxiety. "We've got an expert coming to rescue you. They'll come in from another entrance and lead you back out with them. You should be out of there in a few hours."

Harry glared in the direction of his cousin's voice. "You couldn't have started with that instead of letting me think I'd be in here for days?"

All he heard was laughter. Harry plopped back to the ground.

"It gets better." Matt's delight at Harry's predicament was

beyond wearing thin. "Guess who the resident mine expert is?"

There was so much glee in Matt's voice that Harry knew the answer. He closed his eyes and gave in to the wave of resignation that hit him. "Magenta's coming to save me."

"This is turning out to be the best laugh I've had since Flynn joined the school musical to impress a girl," Matt said.

Harry resisted the urge to bang his head on the wall as he listened to his cousin laugh at his expense. For the first time since he'd made the decision to relocate to Invertary, Harry wondered at the wisdom of coming home.

CHAPTER 4

Magenta arrived at the north-facing entrance of the mine to find a crowd had started to gather. She wasn't surprised. The folk of Invertary were bred nosey. She dumped her backpack with her spelunking gear at her feet and sighed. This was not how she'd planned to spend her Saturday afternoon.

"Who's the idiot who ignored the signs?" she asked Matt.

Apart from the huge red one that said, *Danger—do not enter,* there were at least half a dozen that told people not to shut the door.

Invertary's entire police force grinned. "Listen."

Magenta frowned but did as she was told. Her heart actually stopped cold in her chest as her jaw fell. A very familiar voice was echoing out of the mine. "Is that Harry?"

Matt nodded. The same stupid grin on his face. "I think he's calculating the mass above his head and the probability of it falling on him before his rescue. He used to mutter like this when he was a kid. He doesn't even realise he's doing it. For years he thought Flynn and I had psychic powers because we knew everything he was thinking."

Magenta frowned at him. She remembered Harry's quirk —one of them—she just hadn't realised that his cousin had used it to tease him. If she'd been younger, if she'd still been Harry's friend, she would have taken issue with Matt.

"Harry's too smart to get trapped in there." She pointed at the old metal door and the many signs around it. "He can read, for a start. What happened?"

Matt cocked a thumb over his shoulder. "That's what happened."

She peered around him to find a gleeful Betty. Magenta wasn't convinced. The woman was under five feet tall, built like a cube and older than dirt. "How did she manage to shut the door? There was a huge rock propping it open."

Betty flexed her puny white arms. "Thor there isn't the only one with muscles."

Matt shrugged his broad shoulders. "Don't make me get a magnifying glass to verify that claim."

Betty cackled at him. Magenta sighed. This was exactly what she didn't need. An afternoon rescuing the man she'd spent the past few weeks avoiding. She narrowed her eyes at Betty. "This was no accident. You planned this."

The old woman was delighted. "I couldn't stand his pathetic attempts at getting your attention. So I helped." She rubbed her hands together. "This should be good."

Before Magenta could take a step towards the woman, Matt's hand shot out to stop her. "Get in line. If I let you at her, I have to let everyone else with prior claim get at her too. I don't have the resources to police that."

"Fine." Magenta pointed at Betty. "I'll deal with you later."

"Bring it on, lassie. I eat children like you for breakfast." She turned her back on Magenta, pulled a smartphone out of her pocket and started to text. No doubt spreading the word of entertainment at the mine.

"I'll go in the northern tunnels," Magenta told Matt. She pointed up into the hills around the town. "It's not far, but the route through the mine is winding. It should take me a couple of hours to get to him. Have you called the council surveyor? The whole entrance needs to be checked before we even try to open the door."

Matt nodded. He ran a hand over his face. "I'm thinking we leave the door shut. The mines aren't safe. People who want a look around can negotiate with the Andersons and go in through their business. I'm sure they won't mind as long as it's not all the time and doesn't affect mushroom production. The people who know what they're doing, like you, can go in through the tunnels."

Magenta shook her head. "I've thought about that. I'm worried kids will use the tunnels to get in if the door is sealed. At least at this entrance you can't get into trouble unless you go deep into the mine. Most of the stuff that's dangerous has been removed, or blocked off." She knew that as fact. She was the one who'd cleared the area. "I know this area is safe, but I can't say the same for any of the other hidden entrances in these hills."

"I'll talk to the surveyor. See if we can't come up with a better way to keep the entrance open."

"I don't think it will take much brain power to think of something better than holding the door open with a big rock."

"Maybe we should look into blocking all the entrances and sealing the mine."

"Good luck with finding them all." Magenta shook her head. "No. It needs to be obvious, safe and policed. That's the only way to stop the curious and the stupid from getting hurt."

Matt opened his mouth to reply, but something behind

her caught his attention. His shoulders slumped. "Hell no," he muttered.

Magenta turned to find her twin best friends, Matt's younger sisters, coming up the path. Megan was carrying two folding chairs and Claire held a large picnic basket.

"We brought snacks," Claire called.

"This isn't a party. Go home." Matt glared at the twins.

"Don't tell us what to do, Don Don," Megan said.

"Don't call me Don Don," Matt said through clenched teeth.

Megan was unfazed. "It's your name. Donald Matthew Donaldson. Suck it up."

Matt muttered something that Magenta couldn't quite catch, but was pretty sure was illegal.

Megan set the chairs up facing the entrance. "Who's trapped, anyway? Anybody we know?"

Magenta took a deep breath. She knew exactly what reaction the news would get. "Harry," she said on a sigh.

Two identical faces shared a secret look. Magenta was one of the few people who could tell the blondes apart. When she wanted to wind them up, she pretended she couldn't. If she really wanted to annoy them, she called them Barbie One and Barbie Two. They gave her identical mischievous smiles.

"You're going to rescue Harry? Now isn't that interesting," Claire said. "Especially seeing as he's been so keen to get you alone since he came back to town."

Magenta glared at them, wishing she had the armour of her usual black Goth outfits to hide behind. Unfortunately, there was no place for mini-dresses and platform boots in the mine.

"Mmm, Harry and Magenta locked together in a tight, dark place," Megan said. "I wonder what could happen?" She turned to her sister. "Bodies rubbing against each other. Whispers in the dark. Good job Magenta is immune to

Harry's charms, isn't it?" She turned back to Magenta. "You are immune, aren't you?" She sat back in her chair and opened a bag of freshly made popcorn.

"You"—Magenta pointed at her—"are supposed to be my friend."

"And you"—Megan pointed back—"need to wake up to what's under your nose. He might be our annoying cousin, but even we can see that he's prime man meat. And he's been following you around with his tongue hanging out. Maybe if you put him out of his misery and did the dirty deed, you'd both be in a much better mood."

"Yuck!" Matt covered his ears. "Don't talk like that. It gives me nightmares. He's your cousin and she's your best friend. You shouldn't be encouraging them. You shouldn't know about anything even remotely connected to dirty deeds. You're both too young to know these things. If I had my way, you two would never go near a man. Ever."

"Yeah, you made that clear when we were growing up," Megan said. "But we're twenty-one, and trust me, we know all about dirty deeds."

"La, la, la," Matt sang as he covered his ears. "I can't hear you. I don't want to hear you. You're making me want to run away screaming."

"Oh, get a grip," Megan said. "You should be thankful we're so normal. After dealing with you, Harry and Flynn, it's a miracle we're still attracted to the opposite sex."

"Exactly." Claire flicked a piece of popcorn at him. "I'm still traumatised over the magazines you kept under your bed."

Matt's head went so red that Magenta thought it might explode. She smothered a grin as she picked up her backpack. "I need to get going. Harry is reciting the periodic table."

She knew for a fact that he only did that when he was

really nervous. She started to walk up the path to where the tunnel entrances were hidden.

"Good luck," Megan called after her. "Don't forget to kiss his boo-boos better."

Magenta shook her head and kept on walking.

CHAPTER 5

Being underground was something Harry's brain couldn't comprehend. Sure, he'd known he was going into the old tin mine to see Magenta, but he'd figured it would be like visiting a cave. A nice, open-plan cave. One that had been there for millions of years. A perfectly safe natural occurrence. The reality was far from the fantasy. He was trapped in a space the size of his bedroom, with very little natural light and evidence all around that this was far from nature's doing. Someone had hacked this mine out of the hill. They'd shored it up with timber. Old timber. Timber that was probably rotting, or being eroded by mites. He was stuck in an old, badly made hole in the ground. Just the thought of it made his palms clammy and his throat close.

"Magenta's on her way." Matt's voice cut through his rising panic. "Couple of hours and she'll get to you. She'll lead you back out through the mine. Don't worry. You're in good hands."

All Harry heard were the words *back through the mine*. No. No way. Not going to happen. "Call her back. She's wasting her time." His voice sounded kind of tinny. "I'm not going anywhere. I'm walking out of that door."

"Don't be a drama queen." His cousin sounded tense. "Magenta knows this mine like the back of her hand."

Harry looked at his hand. How well did anyone know the back of their hand? If he closed his eyes he couldn't bring up an accurate image of his, and he saw it millions of times a day. Matt's words were not reassuring.

"I've done the calculations," he told his cousin. "If this comes down on me, there won't be a body for you to recover. I'll be pulverised."

There was a pause. He could almost see Matt rubbing his jaw and muttering for extra strength. "You got any alcohol in that picnic basket Betty made you pack?"

"Wine." Red, white and sparkling. He didn't know what Magenta drank, so he'd covered the bases. He also had bottled water and a set of miniature cans of juice and soda. The damn basket was almost as big as a car. Harry had been pleased that years of workouts meant he could carry the thing.

"Good," Matt said. "Pop the cork on a bottle and start drinking. It would make us all a lot more comfortable if your super brain was fuzzy."

"You're worried what I might do in here, aren't you?"

"Harry." Matt sounded resigned. "You reprogrammed a car when you were six years old. We didn't even know a car could be programmed."

If Harry had been outside the mine, he would have smacked his cousin upside his head. "I don't know if you've noticed, Matt, but there are no cars in here."

"Yeah, I know that, moron, but I'm worried you'll hatch a plan to dig your way out. Or set about reorganising your surroundings to make escape more efficient. I don't want you involved. I want you to let the problem go. We're dealing with it. Your job is to be the damsel in distress. Sit back, look pretty and wait to be rescued."

Harry decided he'd deal with the "damsel in distress" dig when he didn't have a hill hanging over his head. "I'm not drinking the wine. I read up on caving before I came in here. It said don't go caving while drunk."

He could practically hear Matt roll his eyes. "You're not caving. You're stuck behind a door, in a room, in a hill. Think of it as a Hobbit house. Imagine you're visiting with Bilbo. Hanging out, having a glass of wine. See? Easy. The Hobbits live in hills, and they're fine."

"You know Hobbits aren't real, right?"

"You're forgetting about Betty." There was a thud, then a yelp. "You hit me again, old woman, and I'm arresting you for assaulting an officer."

Betty's cackle was loud and clear.

"Drink the wine," Matt said. "One glass won't hurt."

Harry thought about it. "Okay. Maybe one glass. But you need to keep me informed about what's happening out there. I don't even have cell phone coverage in here. I can't get internet access to do any research."

"I swear your mother plugged your toes into a socket when you were born. It's the only reason I can come up with for your obsession with all things electrical. Your head won't explode if you don't have access to a computer for a few hours. Drink your wine and wait for Magenta to get you out."

"I'm not going back through the mine. I'm waiting here until that door opens."

"Whatever," Matt said. "You can work that out with Magenta. I'm sure she'll be very understanding."

Harry thumped back onto the dusty floor, pulled the basket towards him and uncorked a bottle of white wine. He didn't care what kind or colour it was. It all tasted the same to him anyway. Like alcoholic fruit juice, or worse, vinegar. He didn't bother with a glass; instead he brought the bottle to his lips and wished he'd thought to bring beer. In between mouthfuls he recited the periodic table, then rattled off his favourite equations. It didn't help. So he worked on his latest programming code instead—speaking it out into the silence. Hoping the noise would fight back the anxiety he knew waited for him in the dark spaces his eyes couldn't penetrate.

MAGENTA FELT the calming peace of darkness enfold her as she entered the old mine. She loved everything about it, from the musty smell of untouched years to the close intimacy of the spaces she had to shimmy through. The silence of the place was an embrace for her senses, soothing her tension and easing her fears. Here, in this private world, she could relax completely. There was no one watching her. No standards to fall short of. There was no pressure to perform, or conform, or reform her personality. She could just be.

She heard Harry before she saw him. He was speaking code. Something he'd always done, his own private language. When she was a child, his soft chatter would make her feel secure, the meaningless words kind of like the babble of a brook that washed over her. Now it had the opposite effect. Harry's deep, husky tones made her insides tingle and her skin vibrate. A disconcerting effect he'd had since he'd ridden back into town. And one she tried to ignore.

He was concentrating so hard that it took him a minute to realise the light from her hardhat had landed on him. The silence was suddenly deafening as he blinked in her direction. Magenta knew better than to shine her light in someone's eyes, but she couldn't move from the sight of him.

He sat propped against the wall, all lean muscle and long limbs. He wore his usual faded jeans and geek T-shirt. This one said: *Physicists do it at the speed of light.* She gnawed her bottom lip to stop from telling him that doing "it" at the speed of light was not an attractive prospect for most women.

"Magenta?" He sounded unsure.

"Who else would it be, Harry?" She pulled a bottle of water from her pack and gulped down half of it. "Were you expecting the dwarves? Thinking they'd come back to reclaim their mine?"

He gave her a dazzling smile. "Lord of the Rings reference. I'm impressed."

Magenta smiled back, because she knew that Harry couldn't see her. He lifted a hand to shield his eyes from the light.

"Think you can stop blinding me now?"

She switched off the light. It took a minute for her eyes to get used to the darkness. There was a faint glow coming in from a couple of cracks beside the door. It gave off enough illumination to make out shapes.

"Get on your feet," she ordered, hoping that the faster she could get him out of there, the faster she could escape him. "We need to get going."

He smiled, and her stomach fluttered. Harry's smile was devastating. Sweet and sexily confident at the same time. He'd lost the guileless look of youth. Now he seemed to know things. Secret things that only a man would know.

"I'm not going anywhere. I'm staying right here until they open that door." He pointed at the door, in case she was confused.

Magenta worked to ignore the power of his smile. She folded her arms over her black T-shirt and black hooded jacket. "Stop messing around, Harry. Get up. We need to go."

"Uh-uh." He shook his head, his floppy honey-brown hair falling into his eyes.

"I'm getting annoyed." She tapped the toe of her black hiking boot. "I came in here to get you out. To do that, you need to come with me."

Even in the dim light she could see Harry's penetrating stare. His pale grey eyes were like a beacon in the darkness. "I'm sorry you made a wasted trip. I'm not going through the mine."

She glared at him, even though she was sure he couldn't see it. "Why the hell not?" She infused the words with every bit of aggravation she felt.

"Because"—Harry lowered his voice, making it rumble through her body—"I've done the calculations and there isn't enough air in the mine. There's more air here." He pointed at the cracks where light seeped in. "See, you can see it getting in. I'm staying where the air is."

Magenta took a deep breath of Harry's precious air and crouched down in front of him. "Harry, that isn't your brain talking. It's fear. You're not being rational. The mine is full of air vents. We won't be going too deep; there will be plenty of air. I've done this a lot. I know what I'm talking about. You don't have to worry."

He stared at her for a moment. Magenta found herself leaning towards him, as though he somehow magically pulled her closer. "It's more logical to stay here."

"That's great, Mr. Spock, but we're heading out. I'm telling you, Harry, there's plenty of air in the tunnels and I'll make sure you get out safely. I've checked these tunnels myself. They aren't in any danger of collapse. Have I ever lied to you?"

His silver eyes met hers in a challenge. "Yeah, you lied to me. You told me I could always count on you. What was that if it wasn't a lie?"

CHAPTER 6

Magenta knelt on the floor beside Harry. Making sure they didn't touch. His words had felt like a knife slicing into her. The cut cold and clean. The pain precise.

"I was thirteen," she said. "Nobody means what they say when they're thirteen."

"I did. I meant everything I said to you when we were kids."

She almost reached for him then. "You're special, Harry. You've always been special. The rest of us will never meet your standards." She took a deep breath and, without thinking, put a hand on his knee. He stilled at her touch, as though the complete focus of his super brain was suddenly on her. She snatched her hand away. "Come on. Let's go home."

"I can't. It doesn't make any sense to move from this spot. The tonnage of rock and dirt increases as you go deeper into the mine. Abandoned mines are notoriously dangerous. Without regular maintenance they're prone to collapse, or flooding, or a build-up in dangerous gasses. The people who made this mine didn't have equipment to survey the hill to make structurally sound decisions. The reinforcements here alone are enough to give an engineer nightmares. I can't go further without a proper assessment. And I can't do that without the correct equipment. I've made a visual survey of this area. I don't like some of the things I see. But I figure my best chance of surviving a cave-in is here, near the entrance, so people can get to me fast to dig me out. Unless, of course, there is a massive sudden collapse, in which case I estimate I'll be pancaked before I can worry about rescue."

Magenta felt her heart sink. "You researched this before you came in here, didn't you?"

"What else was I supposed to do?"

"Please tell me you didn't read Wikipedia and believe everything in it."

"Do I look like an idiot? I checked the NSS website."

"The American caving group." She hung her head. "You prepared for this, didn't you? Where's your backpack?"

He pointed to the corner. She didn't even have to look in it to know that the contents would be the recommended list he'd found on the website.

"You do know we're not actually caving, right? We're in a mine. The entrance of a mine."

He folded his arms over his broad chest, making his shoulders bulge. For a second she had an urge to bite them. Hard. She shook it off.

"Mines are worse than caves. Solution caves are the safest caves by far. The water cuts through the limestone so slowly that they are really stable. Old and stable. They hardly ever collapse. Do you have any idea how often old mines collapse?"

She didn't, but she was pretty sure Harry did. "Get a grip, Harry. You're being irrational. This mine is safe. I've been coming here for years. I wouldn't lead you into danger. Stop being a wimp and get your backside in gear. I've got better things to do than coax you into leaving."

He folded his arms and gave her that same stubborn look he'd given her when they were kids. "You go. I'll stay." He gestured to the basket. "I have food. Water. More than enough for two days."

Magenta dug her fingers into her hair and tugged it. "I can't leave you here. I'm the rescue. I came in here to get you."

"Thanks. I mean it. I appreciate the effort. But I'm staying right here."

Magenta shot to her feet. The urge to kick him was strong. "You have got to be the most infuriating man on the planet. You've been harassing me to talk to you for weeks, and here I am. All you have to do is walk out with me and we can talk all the way back through the mine." She snatched her bag up from the ground. "This is your last chance. You need to get up and follow me or I'm leaving without you. And you can kiss goodbye to any chat we might have."

He rested his head on the wall behind him and closed his eyes. Resignation came off him in waves.

"I'm going." She put her hat back on and flicked the light on. "Last chance."

He didn't say anything. Magenta suspected he was doing calculus in his head. "Fine. Stay here. Enjoy your two days alone."

With that, she stormed back into the tunnel she'd come out of. Her anger and frustration made her want to hit out at the walls of her sanctuary. Then she heard it. A whisper on the air. Harry.

"I wish you'd stay with me, Magenta."

Instinct told her that she wasn't supposed to hear him. The acoustics of the mine had carried the words to her. It was his tone that melted her anger. She couldn't remember ever hearing such need.

Mentally kicking herself, she turned around. Back to the one man she'd fought to keep away from.

HARRY WASN'T DRUNK. He wasn't even buzzed. At six foot two and two hundred pounds, he knew exactly how much alcohol he needed to drink to get an effect. He was nowhere near it. Sure, he was a little more relaxed than usual. But considering how close he'd been to clawing his way out with his nails, being relaxed was a good thing. One thing he knew for sure: it would take at least another bottle of wine before he got over the ache of Magenta walking away from him. Even though all the official guidelines for being in a situation like this said that alcohol made things worse, he reached for the half-empty bottle of white wine.

"Don't even think about it."

His heart stilled at the voice as a wave of hope almost knocked him over. His eyes shot to the direction Magenta had disappeared. He could make out her black silhouette against the wall. She threw her pack to the floor beside him.

"I'm not hanging out in here with a drunk guy."

He had to swallow twice before he could talk. "So you're staying?" He was glad he didn't sound pathetically grateful.

She let out an exasperated sigh. "You might be a genius out there, but in here you're a bloody idiot. It'd be like leaving a baby to play with a box of matches."

"You're forgetting. It's been eight years since we hung out together. I'm not the kid you knew." Harry grinned at her. "I'm not completely helpless. I have skills."

"Name one that doesn't involve a computer."

"I fight. Mixed martial arts."

"That will be handy when the shadows attack. Try again."

"I can make a fire."

He could almost hear her roll her eyes. "Where would the smoke go, boy genius?"

He hadn't said he *would* make a fire, only that he could.

"See." Magenta plopped down beside him. "You're useless without me."

Harry couldn't have agreed more. He'd known when he was seventeen that he would always be less without Magenta. The years hadn't changed that belief, and spending time around the adult version of his childhood friend had only reinforced it. She'd grown up into his idea of perfect. From her soft, lean figure, with enough curves to make his mouth water, to that prickly attitude and cutting wit, everything about her delighted the man he'd become.

Magenta eyed the basket beside him. "You got anything in there apart from wine?"

"Hungry?"

"Well, I missed dinner to come rescue an idiot who let an old woman trick him into getting trapped in a mine."

Harry ignored that comment. He was beginning to think that Betty's reputation as an evil genius was well deserved. The woman had promised him time alone with Magenta, and that's what he'd gotten. Seemed to him that being trapped in the dark, under a hill, was a small price to pay.

He watched as Magenta strode to a spot near the door. She wasn't wearing her usual uniform of black mini-dress and black platform boots—although she still had on about a tonne of eyeliner. Instead she was dressed for the mine in a black T-shirt and black jeans. Harry vaguely wondered if she owned anything that wasn't black. With her sleek Cleopatra-style hair and her golden eyes, she'd look mouth-watering in pale blue silk. He made a mental note to buy her a sleek silk dress. Then, of course, he'd have to figure out a way to get her into it. He grinned. He was more than up to the challenge. He'd taken on the UK government. Magenta would be a breeze.

"Matt," Magenta shouted.

"I'm here."

"There's been a change of plans. Harry won't leave, so I'm staying until you get the door open. I can't leave him in here alone. It isn't safe."

It was clear from her tone that she wasn't pleased about this news.

"If you knock him out, can you drag his stupid backside out of there?"

Harry frowned at his cousin's words. Magenta looked over at him.

"No can do. He's a big guy for a nerd."

"I work out," Harry said helpfully. "I rock climb. I like hills. But I prefer to be on the outside of them." He could just make out Magenta's frown.

"What if he drinks a lot more wine?" Matt sounded hopeful.

Magenta sighed. "You and I both know that there isn't enough alcohol in the world to stop Harry's brain." Harry liked that comment a lot. It meant she felt like she still knew him. Her belief they had a connection was exactly right, and something he could use to his advantage. Harry grinned at the thought. With the puzzle of Magenta to deal with, he didn't have time to worry about the mine. His brain was full of gorgeous Scottish woman instead.

"You don't need to stay with him," Matt said.

Harry's shoulders tensed. If Matt talked her out of spending two whole days alone with him, he'd string his cousin from a tree.

Magenta sighed and rubbed her temples. "I can't leave an amateur alone in the mine. Plus, you and I both know how much trouble he can cause when he's left unsupervised."

"Hey, I'm not a kid anymore," Harry complained. He didn't like that Magenta saw him as one. He was all man. Her man. He frowned as he planned a way to make her see that.

"Fine." Matt sounded annoyed. "What do you need? I'll have the twins fetch it."

"I've got everything. I leave supplies in here in case I want to spend the night." She looked at Harry. "Or in case I have to spend time down here with someone who's injured or stuck. We're fine for a couple of days. If you can't get the door open by then, we'll have to go to plan B."

Harry couldn't resist. He had to ask. "What's plan B?"

Magenta folded her arms. "A tranquiliser shot. Enough to make you comply, but not enough to knock you out."

Harry burst out laughing. "Yeah, good luck getting near me with a needle."

He could have sworn he heard her growl.

"There will be someone out here around the clock in case you need anything. Shout if you do," Matt said.

"I need my head examined, that's what I need," Magenta muttered.

She walked back over to Harry and plopped to the ground beside him. "Feed me," she ordered.

Harry couldn't contain his grin as he pulled the picnic basket towards them.

As HARRY STARTED EMPTYING the basket, Magenta reached into her pack and retrieved the low-energy lantern. It had the same sort of output as a couple of candles, which was more than enough light to see what they were doing. Unfortunately, it also meant she could see Harry clearly.

His broad shoulders flexed as he unpacked the picnic. His face held pure delight. The same look she'd seen as a kid every time he'd told her about something else he'd discovered. It sent a pang of longing through her that was so intense it was painful.

"Sandwiches, salads, meats, fruit, cake, cookies, crackers, cheese…" He grew more excited with each item he unpacked.

"What are you doing in here with a picnic basket? And how many people were you planning to feed?" Magenta nabbed a chocolate chip cookie.

"Only us."

His big eyes caught hers and her breath stuttered. "The picnic was for me?"

He nodded without breaking eye contact. "I didn't plan to eat in here. I thought we'd sit outside under a tree. Betty said you were taking photos and suggested I surprise you with food."

The cookie was dry in her mouth. She swallowed hard. She wasn't sure what surprised her more: the fact he'd brought her food or the fact he'd taken advice from Betty. "Consider me shocked as hell."

He gave her that sexy smile that made her mouth water, and Magenta had a hard time returning her attention to the food.

"You didn't plan on being in the mine, but you packed an emergency bag?"

He shrugged. "Always be prepared. Boy Scout motto."

"You were kicked out of the Boy Scouts after you blew up their hut."

"Yeah, they weren't prepared for that." His delighted grin almost made her laugh.

Magenta chewed the cookie thoughtfully. "Want to tell me why you were bringing me food when I told you clearly that I have no intention of restarting a friendship with you?"

There was a moment of silence as she became the focus of Harry's full attention. Part of her wanted to jump up and run. She fought to stay still. To listen to what he had to say to her.

Slowly, those silver eyes of his turned black. "I totally agree. I don't think we can be friends."

Magenta felt disappointment overwhelm her, even though this was what she wanted.

"I don't want to be friends." Harry's deep voice rumbled over her. "I want to be more than that. I brought the food in the hope it would appease you. You see"—he leaned towards her—"I needed you in a good mood, because I planned to seduce you."

Magenta choked on her cookie.

CHAPTER 7

Harry could have sworn he heard a muffled cheer. He would have investigated, but he didn't care about the strange noises in the mine. He cared about Magenta. He grabbed a bottle of water and thrust it at her. He patted her back and hoped he wouldn't have to perform the Heimlich manoeuvre. At last she had seemed to bring herself under control.

"That wasn't funny," she said.

"I wasn't joking."

There was silence while Magenta stared at him and Harry tried to figure out what she was thinking. His whole world telescoped to include just her. She was beautiful. With her wide eyes, heart-shaped face and skin as smooth as cream. No. Beautiful wasn't the right word. Unfortunately, he didn't know of a better one. She was the walking, talking version of Einstein's equation for general relativity. That's how perfect she was.

At last she put her hand on his arm, licked her full bottom lip and blinked up at him.

"I'm sorry, but I don't think about you that way."

If he hadn't been prepared for that response, it would have felt like a punch to the gut.

"No, you probably don't *consciously* think about me like that. But you *are* attracted to me. That's why I planned to seduce you. I want to *make* you think of me that way."

Her hand fell away. She stood and paced away from him.

"Stop messing around, Harry. I'm not attracted to you. I don't even want to talk to you." The fact she blushed and couldn't look him in the eye spoke volumes. She was lying. He just wasn't sure why.

"Your pupils dilate with desire when I'm near you." He stood slowly, his focus on Magenta. "You lick your lips when you talk to me. As though you're getting ready for me to taste them." He prowled slowly towards her. In his mind she was prey. His prey. And she wasn't getting away. Not this time. Not ever. He lowered his voice, making his tone a caress. Watching her shiver in response. "You cross your arms in an attempt to barricade yourself from me, but it never lasts long. Instead you stroke the inside of your wrist, as though you want me to touch you there. You tuck your hair behind your ear when you look at me. It's an unconscious show of your femininity. An attempt to make yourself more desirable to me." He kept her in his sights. "You can't make yourself more desirable to me. It's impossible. The desire I feel already consumes me."

She retreated from him until her back hit the wall behind her. She held out her hand, palm facing him, and all he could think about was kissing it. Or making a circle with his tongue. How would she taste? Sweet? Spicy?

He moved steadily towards her. "Your cheeks flush when you're near me. I wonder what other parts of your body flush for me too." At last he was in her space. They weren't touching, but he was close enough to feel the heat coming from her much smaller body. Without her usual platform boots the top of her head came to under his chin, and he knew that she would tuck against him perfectly.

"Your heart beats faster when I'm around." He ran a finger down her jaw line. A faint sigh of a touch. Her breathing stuttered. "I see it pounding here." He gently caressed the vein at the curve of her jaw that always betrayed her desire. "Your stomach clenches when you try to dismiss me." The backs of his fingers brushed her cheek. Skin so smooth it was porcelain under his touch. "Your hand often flattens on your stomach, as though you're trying to ease the tension."

She put a hand on his chest to stop him. It seared.

"I'm not some body-language test case from a book you read." Her voice was breathless.

"Am I wrong, though?"

She let out a grumpy-sounding sigh. "Okay, you win. I'll admit, I think you look good. I'd have to be blind not to notice the way you've turned out. Half the women in town are drooling over you. Even if I did find you attractive, it doesn't mean I want to do anything about it. I find Lake attractive, but he's marrying Kirsty. See? Attraction doesn't mean anything."

As his hand softly, gently moved to clasp the back of her neck, he leaned towards her ear. His voice a whisper against her skin. Her breathing strained now. "You want me as much as I want you. And I want you more than I want my next breath."

"I don't want you." She didn't sound convinced.

"Are you sure? Wouldn't you like to touch just this once? Kiss one time? If only to see what would happen. I bet it would be explosive. Every time you're around me I feel the air ionise. I know touching you, being touched by you, will blow my mind. Don't you want to see if I'm right?"

"We're not even friends," she whispered. Her golden eyes were wide, beseeching him to understand.

"We've always been much more than friends." His words feathered across her cheek to her lips. "We were meant for each other, Magenta mine. We just lost our way."

Her fingers fisted in his T-shirt. "We didn't lose our way. You went to university. You left me."

"I'm here now."

Gently, softly, he touched his lips to Magenta's mouth.

CHAPTER 8

Time froze for Magenta. She found herself paralysed by Harry's touch. As his sensual mouth teased her lips, she felt the tightly sealed box within her crack. Teenage memories of wanting Harry seeped through the gap. She'd been thirteen and desperate for him to notice her as a girl. Desperate for him to touch her. But he never did. Instead he'd left Invertary. Left her behind to defend herself at school. Left her alone without him. Aching for him.

"Stop it." Harry's word rumbled against her lips. "The past is gone. This is now."

Harry hadn't lost his knack for reading her mind, and with those words he pulled her back into the present. She felt his large hand span the small of her back, pressing her body flush against him. He was a solid wall of strength, his muscles vibrating with restraint as he held her firmly but gently.

Her brain had short-circuited. Kissing Harry was a teenage dream come true. A dream she found herself indulging in, even though common sense told her to stop before she got hurt. Her hand curled tighter into his T-shirt. His tongue brushed across the seam of her lips, making her weaken. A gasp escaped. Harry took advantage, angling his mouth so that he could taste all of her. Claim all of her.

Her body melted against his as she let him take control. The taste of him was a feast for her senses. She felt the blood rush through her veins and bubble with erotic effervescence. The air swirled around her. Somehow, being in the darkness and stillness of the mine, being in a place she thought of as hers alone, made the intimacy increase tenfold.

His lips moved from her mouth to her neck, teasing kisses down to the curve of her shoulder. He bit her gently before sucking her skin into his mouth. She heard herself whimper and didn't care.

"You are so freaking delicious." The words were a vibration against her skin.

He traced his tongue up to her ear before nibbling her earlobe. "I want to eat you all up." His desire was little more than a low, rumbling breath against her ear that sent shivers rippling through her body.

His scent overwhelmed her, filling her head with romance-novel images of sun-kissed fields and Harry bare-chested in faded jeans. She was losing her mind. Becoming some weak, girly person who ached for a man—and she didn't care. In fact, she wanted to float away on the feelings he induced in her. Float away and never return.

Harry's huge hand engulfed her breast and made her ache. There was too much material between them. She wanted it gone. Now. His thumb teased her nipple, and Magenta growled into his mouth. More. She wanted more. Needed more. All thoughts of keeping away from Harry were gone from her head. All that was left were the loud, desperate pleas of her body. And all her body wanted was Harry.

"More," she ordered.

Harry complied. His hand swept under her T-shirt and

back to her breast. She made a noise of complaint. Her bra was still between them.

"You feel better than I ever imagined," he said against her lips. "I want you in my mouth."

Yes. She pressed into him. That was what she wanted too. More than she wanted to breathe.

"What's happening in there? Are you kissing? Please tell me you're kissing."

The excited voice of her friend cut through the moment, bringing Magenta back from the warm outdoors and into the dusty mine where Harry was clutching her closely, his fingers teasing her breast. His breathing laboured. His heartbeat a thud against her skin.

"Go away," he growled at his cousin.

Magenta's brain was struggling to process the interruption. Part of her couldn't understand why Harry had stopped kissing her. It was the same part of her that wanted to throw him to the ground and jump on top of him.

"Harry?" one of the twins said. "You sound all He-Man, Master of the Universe."

"I should never have loaned them those comics," Harry mumbled against Magenta's ear, making it tingle.

A cold wave of reality washed over Magenta. She stiffened in Harry's arms. He softly kissed her cheek, aware the moment was shattered.

"Magenta?" It was one of the twins again. "What's happening? We need to know."

Magenta pushed away from him, tugging her T-shirt back down. She kept her eyes from Harry.

"Harry, honey"—that had to be Claire—"what's going on in there?"

Magenta had pulled herself together enough to glare a threat at him. He'd better not tell anyone anything. He cocked an eyebrow like he was amused by her silent demand.

With his eyes still on her, he opened his mouth to speak. Magenta clenched her fists.

"Magenta and I are working out our differences," he told his cousins. "Not that it's any of your business, but there was definitely kissing. Great kissing, and there would have been even more if you two hadn't stuck your noses in."

As the twins squealed with delight, Magenta clenched her teeth tightly. "There is nothing going on here." She was pleased her voice didn't sound breathless and needy. "I don't know what that was"—she pointed at the wall where he'd held her—"but it wasn't kissing. I felt nothing."

"You felt nothing?" Harry gave her a cocky smile. "Well, I need to try harder next time, then."

"There will be no next time. That was a mistake."

He gave her a look that said he clearly believed otherwise, and she fought the urge to kick him in the shin.

"What do you mean mistake?" a twin asked. "Did Harry trip over and his lips hit yours? How can you accidentally kiss?"

"Yeah, Magenta, tell dumb and dumber how you accidentally clung to me while I made you moan." He folded his arms over his wide chest. He was mocking her.

"There was moaning?" Megan wailed.

"Get away from there," Matt said. "This unhealthy interest you have in your cousin's sex life is disturbing."

"There is no sex," Magenta shouted. "And if Harry comes near me again, there will be no life either."

He laughed at her threat.

Magenta stomped over to where she'd left her flashlight. "I'm going to get supplies for tonight." She pointed at Harry. "Don't go anywhere."

"Don't worry. This is exactly where I want to be."

Magenta wanted to smack the smug smile off his face. She growled with frustration as she headed into the mine, to where she kept a locked trunk full of equipment. Part of her wanted to run back through the mine to the tunnel entrance and leave Harry to deal with things on his own. A bigger part of her, the more sensible, responsible part, couldn't do that to him.

She told herself that her resolve to stay with him had absolutely nothing to do with the fact her heart still raced and her lips were still swollen from his touch. It also had nothing to do with how needy her body felt. Or how desperate her skin was to be touched again.

No, her decision to stay had nothing to do with any of that. Nothing at all.

CHAPTER 9

Harry whistled happily while Magenta disappeared into the mine.

"Magenta, Harry?" His cousin's voice broke through Harry's cheer. "I hate to break up the party, but I have good news and bad news."

Harry turned towards the voice. "Magenta's gone into the mine to get her gear. Tell me. Bad news first."

"Actually, it's only one piece of news. It's good and bad."

"Okay, genius, give me the *only* news."

"The council engineer has arrived and he's brought a new piece of equipment with him. It looks like a huge motorised jack. He says he can get the door open now. He'll use the jack to prop up the entrance beams until he's had a chance to look at it properly tomorrow."

Harry's heart stopped beating. He was technically dead. And he was in hell.

"Did you hear me?" Matt said. "We can have you out of there within the hour. Your time to seduce Magenta by playing the damsel in distress is over. Sorry, cuz."

Harry's huge brain went into overdrive. "It's starting to

get dark—wouldn't it be better to try this tomorrow, when the guy can see properly?"

"He's come with floodlights. Plus he told me he was out here a couple of weeks ago, did a thorough inspection of the entrance and he's certain it won't collapse when the door opens. He only brought the jack thing as a precaution."

"Tell him I'll spring him a night at the hotel, and pay his tab at the bar while he's there, if he waits until morning."

He definitely heard a cheer this time. He shook his head in wonder.

"I like the way you think, son," Betty called.

"Back off, Betty," Matt said. "This is police business."

Harry heard Betty's grumbling become faint as she uncharacteristically did as she was told.

"How many people are out there?" Harry said.

"There's a crowd. The twins went home for a tent. They're parking here for the night because they don't want to miss anything. Looks like others are going to do the same. Every noise you make is coming out of the mine loud and clear. And I mean *every* noise. You sure you want to stay in there for the night? You won't get much privacy."

Harry thought it through. Magenta was scared as a rabbit at the dog track. If he let her get away from him now, he wasn't sure when he'd be able to corner her again. He weighed the odds in his head. Missing his chance by leaving the mine straight away, or dealing with a furious Magenta when she found out everyone heard her personal business. He picked a night with Magenta. Although he did hope she didn't chase him with a shotgun when she found out they'd spent the night in the mine needlessly.

"We're staying here," he told Matt.

There was definitely a cheer this time.

"Are you sure you know what you're doing?" Matt wasn't convinced.

"Yeah. I'm sure. I'm not leaving here until Magenta knows she's mine."

"You are seriously deranged. She's going to take a rusty knife to your balls when she finds out."

Without conscious thought, Harry's hand shot down to protect his fly. That sounded way worse than a shotgun.

"Can you do something to the vent, give us a bit more privacy?"

There was booing.

"I'll see what I can do." Matt sounded resigned. "You realise you've grabbed a tiger by its tail?"

Harry grinned. "Don't worry. I plan to play with the whole cat." He heard footsteps echo through the tunnel behind him. "She's coming back. Talk to the engineer. Buy us the night."

"It's your funeral. The engineer will be back first thing in the morning. I can't believe I'm doing this."

"Don't freak out on me. This isn't illegal. You're still a good cop."

"Yeah, but as a cousin I need to have my head examined for letting you talk me into this."

"When you find your soul mate, I'll help you out."

"Not going to happen." Matt's words had such finality that they made Harry laugh.

"Who are you talking to?" Magenta said behind him.

Harry turned towards her and, as usual, the rightness of seeing her slammed him in the chest. "Matt. There's good news. The engineer can get us out in the morning."

Her shoulders relaxed slightly. "Good. That's good. One night is more than enough."

"I hope so," Harry said under his breath.

CHAPTER 10

It was hard to ignore Harry in the intimate darkness of the mine, but Magenta tried her best. Her body had been sensitised by his touch, to the point where she was painfully aware of the still air around her. Before Harry had left for university, and Magenta had realised she'd developed a crush on her best friend, she'd daydreamed about kissing him. They'd been the dreams of a child. Chaste kisses, timid touches. Him holding her gently. Nothing like the reality of kissing Harry the man. There was nothing timid about the grown-up version of her childhood crush. He was confident, sexy and mind-blowingly skilled. So much so that the need to repeat the experience almost crushed the shock she had over kissing him in the first place.

However much she wanted to kiss him again, she had to resist. There was no future for them. He was a computer genius, a guy with two doctorates and a multimillion-dollar business. She was a high school dropout who sold underwear for a living. She'd known back in school that they were worlds apart. She was far too stupid for Harry. A fact her schoolmates had taken every opportunity to rub in. A fact her mother had reinforced whenever she could. She looked at the man who made her lose her mind, and shivered. All she had to do was resist him until the morning. Then, when the door opened, they'd both go back to their completely separate lives.

"We might as well get ready for bed." As soon as the words were out of her mouth, she wished them back.

"I'm all yours." She felt Harry's smile zing through her body like a ball in a pinball machine. To fend off her rebellious hormones—the ones that wanted her to rub up against Harry like a cat in heat—she recited a mantra in her head. *I will not kiss Harry. I will not touch Harry. I will not lick Harry.*

It didn't help

"I mean." She tucked her hair behind her ear, before remembering what he'd told her about that gesture. "We need to get the place prepared for sleeping." She pointed to the gear she'd dragged back with her. "I have sleeping bags and mats."

Harry pushed away from the wall, where he'd been leaning, and picked up his backpack. "I brought a tent."

Magenta stilled, sleeping bag in hand. At last something had managed to distract her from Harry's effect on her body. "You brought a tent? To a mine?" She stared at him. "You do know we're already indoors, right?"

"The tent isn't to keep the elements out. It's to keep the vermin out." He shuddered as he said the word. "Rats, mice and bats. They're biochemical weapons with feet and teeth. Hence the tent."

Magenta dropped the sleeping bag and stared at the man. Tall, broad, muscled, with an air of danger, Harry wasn't your typical geek. He also didn't look like he'd have nightmares over Mickey Mouse.

"Are you scared?" She could hardly believe it possible.

"Hell yes. I'm not ashamed to admit it. It takes courage

to face a fear. Or in this case, hide from it in a rat-proof tent. What do you do about the rats when you're down here?"

She shrugged. "I go to sleep and hope they don't bother me. If something comes sniffing around, I wake up and scare it off."

He cringed as she spoke. "They have germs. They have sharp little teeth and no awareness of personal space. Do you know how many deadly viruses are in the saliva of a bat? Or a rat? Any rodent at all? One bite and it's adios, amigo. Trust me, in this case, prevention is way better than cure. We're sleeping in the tent."

Magenta narrowed her eyes at him. Really? He was ordering her around? The guy had a death wish. "You can sleep in the tent. I'll sleep out here."

He folded his arms in an attempt to intimidate her. It didn't work. "We're both sleeping in the tent. Otherwise I'll stay awake all night long worrying that you're being eaten alive by rats."

"And that's my problem how? Stay awake if you want. You're the one with the irrational fear. I've slept in here before. I'm fine. You can have the tent."

He studied her for a moment. "I tell you what. We'll play a game, and if I win, you sleep in the tent, where you'll be safe from catching the plague. Yep, you heard right. The plague. As in 'wipes out entire continents' plague. If you win you can sleep out here. Of course, I'll have to stay awake all night to make sure nothing comes near you, but that's a sacrifice I'm willing to make."

"You're one big walking, talking psychologist's wet dream. You can't go in the mine because there's too much dirt above your head and not enough air. You can't sleep in a perfectly dry and secure room because the baby mice might eat you. Is there anything else I should know while I'm stuck in here with you? Any more irrational fears that will drive me insane?"

"Worrying about a cave-in and lack of air isn't irrational. It's logical. We're not talking about pet mice you buy in a pet store. They're the sanitised version. Although I still wouldn't let them near me. We're talking about the hard-core, bug-infested, rabid rodents from hell. That's what we're talking about. There's nothing irrational about fearing those. Nothing. Wise people take sensible precautions. Like sleeping in a tent. Away from the rats."

Magenta rubbed her temples. She didn't remember him being this much work when they were kids. But she'd never been stuck underground with him then, either. She tried a different tactic.

"Hobbits live in man-made holes in the ground and they don't worry about rats or sleep in tents."

He cocked an eyebrow at her. "What is it with this town and its obsession with Hobbits?"

"It was worth a try," Magenta mumbled.

"Either we play the game and settle this, or we spend the night discussing it. It's your call. I can tell you right now, I have an encyclopaedic knowledge of everything that can go wrong when you confront a rodent, and I'm more than happy to share that knowledge with you—all night long."

"Fine." She ground her teeth together. "What game do you want to play? Don't even think about suggesting strip poker."

The dazzling smile was back. "I don't have any playing cards." He actually sounded sad at that. "How about I draw a circle over there." He pointed at the entrance to the tunnels. "We'll keep it simple. We'll each take turns throwing a stone. The one who gets it closest to the middle of the circle wins."

"Seriously. That's your game?"

"You got a better idea?"

"Draw the damn circle. Let's get this over with."

Harry grinned, grabbed a piece of limestone from the floor beside him and trotted over to draw on the dusty ground. The circle he drew was teensy. Barely bigger than the size of her fist.

"That's the size we're aiming for? Are you sure you don't want to make it smaller?"

He studied the drawing for a minute. "No. It's perfect."

"How many turns each?"

"One should be enough, don't you think?"

Magenta stared at him. "I can't tell you how much I don't care. Are you sure about this? I seem to remember you being rubbish at any sort of ball game when we were kids."

He gave her a cheeky look that made her blush. "I keep telling you, Magenta. I'm not a kid anymore."

He bent down in front of her, making her sway at the nearness of him. He drew a line in the ground. "We'll both throw from here." He pointed at the line.

"Fine. Whatever. Let's get this over with. You go first."

She huffed in frustration as Harry took years to pick the perfect stone. At last, he stepped behind the line and lobbed the stone at the circle. It landed with perfect precision close to the centre of the circle. He gave her a cocky smile.

"My aim has improved since we last played," he said, oozing confidence.

Magenta picked up a huge boulder from beside her feet. It took two hands to throw it. It landed with a loud thud, obliterating the circle and Harry's stone. She dusted off her hands and grinned.

"I think it's safe to say that mine is closer to the centre of the circle."

Harry's mouth opened and closed several times before he spoke. "That doesn't count. You cheated."

She shrugged. "You should have been more specific about

the rules. Now that's over, we can sleep outside the tent. Like normal people."

"You mean *you* can sleep outside the tent. I'll be standing guard."

"Whatever you want to do. I don't care. I'm tired and I'm going to sleep. Enjoy your rat watch."

HARRY SET up his tent and sat in the entrance of it, his flashlight aimed at Magenta. He thought he'd win the game. He thought he'd be tucked up tight with his girl in his tent. He should have picked a game she couldn't cheat at. It brought back all the memories he had of her outwitting him as a kid, and it made him grin with delight. Magenta had always been a challenge.

"Will you turn that damn light off? Every time you sweep it over the room it wakes me up." Magenta was wrapped up tight in her sleeping bag, her back to the wall beside Harry. He'd been watching her closely. She was lying. There was no way she'd been asleep.

"I'll keep it away from your eyes." There was no way he was doing that, either. If he couldn't get her into his tent and pressed up against him fair and square, he wasn't above aggravating her into doing what he wanted.

He waited to speak until her breathing started to even out as she slipped into a light sleep. "Did you know that in Vietnam, you can eat barbecued rats? That's dicing with death. You could be eating typhus, trichinosis, salmonellosis or rat-bite fever. I'm no expert, but I'm pretty sure even barbecuing won't kill those bugs. Does that sound like a healthy meal to you?"

He stifled a grin as Magenta groaned. "I wish I'd thought to pack earplugs. Shut up, Harry, and let me sleep."

"I can't help it. Whatever is in my brain slips out of my mouth."

She growled something he couldn't hear, then turned to face the wall. Again Harry waited until her breathing indicated she was falling asleep.

"There are over seventy million rats in New York City. I don't think there's that many down here, but I bet there are thousands."

"Harry!" She propped herself up on an elbow, turned her head and glared at him. "I am this close to killing you. If you want to get out of here alive, you need to stop talking."

"I'll try harder."

He made sure the light of his flashlight danced over her while she tried to sleep as he prepared his next rat fact. "Rat mothers often eat their young. They're cannibals. And incestuous. Mothers mate with sons. It's disgusting."

"That's it!" Magenta jumped to her feet. She pointed at Harry. "You are driving me insane. If you don't stop talking about rats, I'm going to find another part of the mine to sleep in."

"Then I'll have to follow you to keep you safe from rodent attack."

"I thought you couldn't go into the mine?"

"My need to keep you safe from rats far outweighs my worry about cave-ins."

She put her hands on her curvy hips and glared. She was barefoot, dressed only in cotton boy shorts and a sports bra, with a large T-shirt on top. All black, as usual. Her hair had lost its sleek edge and her face was makeup free. She was stunning. The golden tone of her skin glowed in the faint light of the room, made even more translucent by the stark blue/black she used to dye her hair. Her golden-brown eyes sparkled with rage, which had the effect of making Harry's libido spike. He shifted uncomfortably in his jeans.

"I don't need you to keep me safe. I'm the one who's here to keep you safe. You're the rank amateur who managed to get stuck in a mine. You're getting on my last nerve with this macho rubbish. There is no such thing as an alpha geek. There's just alpha. And geek. You're a geek."

"Baby." Harry smiled, hoping it would disarm her. "I'm a muscled geek. Look." He lifted his T-shirt to flash his abdomen. "I have a two-pack. That's two more than most geeks have."

He looked down. Hey, who knew? It had morphed into a four-pack. He grinned at Magenta, stilling as he saw the heat in her eyes. Part of him wanted to preen with male pride. The other part of him, the one that was into self-preservation, told him to stop pushing the Goth. He let his shirt drop.

"I don't need anyone to look after me." She folded her arms, which he supposed was meant to be intimidating but instead made him stare at her breasts. "I've been looking after myself just fine for years."

"Okay." Harry held up his hands in surrender. "How about you humour me? I hate flea-infested, virus-ridden rodents. We'd both sleep a lot better if I didn't have to spend the night worrying that they were out to get us." He pointed at the tent. "What harm can it do? We both know you're big and brave enough to sleep out here. But what if I need protecting? Sleep in the tent with me, Magenta, and keep me safe from the rats." He batted his eyelashes at her and hoped it worked.

He could practically see her thinking. "Damn it. You are a huge pain in my backside." She bent over to pick up her sleeping bag and mat, giving Harry a mouth-watering view of her heart-shaped rear.

"Get in the bloody tent before I change my mind."

He didn't need to be told twice. Scooting back, he lay on top of his sleeping bag and patted the space he'd left beside him for Magenta. "Get yourself sorted, and then I'll lock up the tent for the night."

She rolled her eyes. "Not worried the rats will chew through the nylon and get to you anyway?"

He grinned. "I sprayed the tent with pine oil before I left. It's poison to rats." That deserved a high-five at least, but he didn't think he'd get one.

"That explains the smell. I feel like I'm surrounded by a giant car air freshener."

She rolled out her bag on to the ground beside him, trying to leave enough of a gap between them to make her feel better. Harry allowed it. He had no plans to let it stay like that.

"Okay, I'm closing up." He reached for the zip. "Want to use the facilities before I shut the door?"

"It's a bucket, Harry."

"Fine. Want to use the bucket before I close the flap?"

"No. I want to go to sleep." She glared at him again. "Are you going to let that happen now?"

"Absolutely." He fastened the flap before stretching out on top of his bag. Once he was certain they were both settled, he flicked off his flashlight. "Night, Magenta."

She growled, and Harry grinned into the pitch-black darkness.

CHAPTER 11

Magenta couldn't sleep. Of course she couldn't sleep. The air between them was thick with everything unsaid. Her body was hyperaware of every move Harry made. And deep inside, she was hungry. Hungry for another touch from him. She rolled over for about the millionth time and pummelled the fleecy jacket she used as a pillow. It didn't help.

"Spock." Harry's voice cut through the darkness. "Iron Man, Bruce Banner, Professor Xavier, Spider-Man, Indiana Jones…"

"Is this the geek equivalent of counting sheep?"

He chuckled. It was nice. A low rumble that made her smile.

"They're all alpha geeks."

She had to work at keeping the amusement out of her voice. "They're also all fictitious."

There was a pause. "I might have to get back to you later if you want a list of real-life alpha geeks."

Magenta snorted. "Yeah, like next century."

She felt Harry lean up and turn towards her. "Are you saying that you can't be manly and intelligent?"

"That's a trick question, right?"

He laughed, and it delighted her. She remembered when they were little and she'd loved to make him laugh. He put his all into it. It made her grin.

"Matt said you're the local expert caver. Said he's been trying to get you to go for your Local Caver and Mine Leader qualification. The twins told him you dreamed of running your own holiday caving business."

Magenta didn't say anything. Seemed like Matt had talked enough about her private business for both of them.

"How come you haven't sat the qualification?"

"Not my thing. Exams never were." She hoped that would shut the discussion down. The truth was that she would kill to have that certificate, but it wasn't possible. Not for her. There was silence for a few minutes. Magenta hoped it would last. No such luck.

"When did the caving start?"

"I used to come up here when I skipped school. It was the one place I was sure no one would look for me." She shrugged even though she knew Harry couldn't see her. "One day I met a couple who were walking the mine. They were cavers, and through them I got into proper caving."

They weren't only cavers. They were lifesavers. She'd met Sally and Graeme when she'd been adrift in life. She couldn't cope in school, which made her act out all the time. She'd honestly believed she was too stupid to do anything, then, just in time, she'd discovered she had a knack for caving and had clung to it like a lifeline.

"You still see this couple?" Harry's voice broke her out of her reminiscing.

"Yeah, I'm part of their caving team. We do a few trips a year."

"Did the photography come from them too?"

"I met up with a group of urban explorers a couple of

years ago. They're like the cavers of man-made things. Not always underground structures, but always abandoned ones. They take pictures and video and post online. I thought of this place and how cool it would be to make a record of it. That's how the photography started."

"You're an urban explorer." He sounded somewhere between intrigued and amused.

"Mainly I'm a caver. But I like this mine. It's my own personal caving system."

She felt Harry move beside her. He was suddenly closer to her, but she wasn't sure he was doing it on purpose, so she let it go.

"I don't like the idea of you down here alone. It's dangerous."

She rolled her eyes. "You're doing that macho crap again, but you're right. The mine *is* dangerous. Usually I would say you never explore anything underground without there being at least three of you. That's what cavers do, they go in teams, but this mine is different. I spent years exploring it as a kid. Sure, I was lucky I never got injured or lost, but it means that no one knows this place better than I do. If someone else came in here on their own, I'd blast them for it. But I know what I'm doing. I know this mine. Plus, I always tell the twins where I'm going and when I expect to get back. That way, if something freaky happens, someone can find me."

"I don't like it." She could have guessed Harry would say that even before the words came out of his mouth.

Magenta couldn't help laughing. "I don't care what you like and don't like, Hairy Boil."

He grunted. "I know, Maggie Fraser."

Without thinking, she swung her arm and smacked him in the vicinity of his stomach. Harry grabbed her hand and held it tightly. Her thoughts stuttered before she remembered she was annoyed. "Don't call me that." She tugged to free her hand. Harry threaded his fingers with hers, and the touch made Magenta hyperaware of her heartbeat.

"Then don't call me Hairy Boil," he said with a laugh.

"Imbecile."

"Tyrant."

Magenta stopped trying to free her hand and decided instead to pretend Harry wasn't holding it. She didn't want to admit to him, or to herself, that she liked it. She liked the feel of his skin against hers. The warmth of his touch. The strength in his hold. She liked it all a little too much.

"You go rock climbing?"

"Yes. Outside. In the air. Where nothing can bury me alive."

"Drama queen," she muttered.

"I'll take you sometime. It utilises some of the same skills as caving, only in daylight."

"Yeah, that's not going to happen."

"I tell you what. I'll go caving with you, if you go rock climbing with me."

She wanted to. She really did. But each step closer to Harry was a step closer to watching him reject her when he discovered her secret. She'd known at thirteen that having Harry judge and reject her would devastate. It would be even worse to have him reject her now that all the potential he'd had as a teenager had been realised. He was sexy, built like a fighter and so freaking confident in his own intelligence that it dazzled. He wasn't easy to resist, but she knew he would leave her broken beyond repair if she let him get close and then watched him turn away.

"How about we don't do either?" She hoped she sounded far cooler than she felt.

Harry chuckled as he let go of her hand. A squeal left her lips as strong hands grasped her hips and lifted her up.

Before she could form words, she was tucked in at Harry's side, her head in the crook of his shoulder, his hand branding her hip.

"What the hell?" She leaned up to face him, even though she couldn't see him in the dark. His grip tightened.

"You were driving us both nuts with your bashing around. You're obviously uncomfortable and worried you'll somehow touch me in your sleep. This way, you're comfortable and you don't have to worry about the touching."

"What if I don't want to be wrapped around you like a pretzel?"

His lips brushed her ear. "Oh, but you do want to be wrapped around me, Magenta," he whispered.

Magenta's mouth went dry as need pulsed through her body. Her sensible, rational mind—the one that reminded her a future with Harry wasn't possible—was overwhelmed by the nearness of him. A small voice whispered in her brain. It told her to take this. This one night close to Harry. She deserved this one chance to touch him, to breathe him in, to feel him surround her, because in the morning, when the door to the mine opened, she'd close the door to her heart for good. "I'll sleep here, but only because it's more comfortable. Don't get any ideas."

"I wouldn't dare." He was mocking her. She knew it.

Stiffly, she placed her head back on his chest. Why did he smell like freaking Christmas? Did he bathe in mulled wine? It made her want to lick him and taste him. Maybe lying next to Harry wasn't such a great idea after all.

Harry's laughter vibrated through her body before she heard it. "You'll never get to sleep if you don't relax."

"How am I supposed to relax when you're this close to me, genius? This doesn't exactly feel natural. I'm not used to touching you like this."

"We used to cuddle all the time when we were kids."

Her cheeks heated at the thought. She'd spent many an evening curled up against Harry watching *Star Trek* on his bedroom TV.

"It isn't the same. You're about twice the size and you're a whole lot firmer. Hotter too."

"You think I'm hot?"

She heard the grin in his voice and rolled her eyes. "I meant body heat. Not attractiveness."

"Whatever you want to believe."

She frowned as she wriggled against him, trying to get the perfect comfy place to sleep. She suspected that position might be her splayed on top of him.

"Lie still."

"I'm trying. This is weird. I can't help that it's freaking me out."

He sighed. "What would make it un-weird?"

"Is un-weird even a word?"

"Magenta." It was a warning.

"Nothing," she said. "Nothing will make it less weird, not until I get used to being near you like this."

His body tensed for a moment. "You're telling me that you need to become more familiar with me in order to sleep?"

"Yeah." She resisted the urge to pummel his shoulder much like she'd pummelled her makeshift pillow. This wasn't going to work. She wriggled in an attempt to get out of his hold.

"Stop that," he ordered. Seriously, the guy needed to get over his ruler-of-the-world mentality. She opened her mouth to tell him so.

"If getting used to me will help you relax," he said, "then that's something I can help with."

She heard it in his words—a low, rumbling sensuality that made her blood fizz with excitement. She stilled, going over the conversation in her head to see what she'd missed. Harry's arm stayed tight around her waist as he turned towards her.

"By the time I'm finished you'll be so comfortable around me, you won't even notice I'm here."

"Harry?" She hated that she sounded more breathless than confused.

He moved over her in the pitch-blackness. She felt his face at the curve of her neck. "It's all about familiarity." He trailed his nose up her skin, breathing deeply. A low growl of approval. "You had no problem sleeping around me years ago. Remember, we'd sit on the hill not far from here? You'd put your head on my knee while I worked on my laptop." She remembered. He'd been fifteen. She'd been twelve and falling in love for the first time—for the only time—with her best friend.

His breath against her ear made her shudder, and she found herself clinging to Harry's shoulders, her nails digging in. She willed her fingers to uncurl, but they wouldn't. They couldn't. "I'd stroke your hair," he whispered. "It was longer then, the colour of manuka honey. And soft." She felt his fingers in her hair at the back of her head. "I've never felt anything softer." His body was over hers, pressing against her. A heavy blanket that made her quiver with sensation.

"I like it black too." She couldn't see him. Only feel him, which somehow made each touch more electric. "It would look even sexier with a hint of blue. Yeah," he said, his fingers twirling a lock of her hair. She knew he couldn't see her any better than she could see him, but she could tell by the way he spoke that he had a picture in his head. "Blue, not pink. Blue-tipped hair, blue silk dress. Ankle length, sleek. No frills, just like you. Thin straps so I can see your shoulders." Gentle fingers trailed over her shoulder, pushing the wide-necked tee along with it until her skin was exposed. Harry curved a hand over her shoulder, blistering her skin with his touch, making her suck in his scent along with a gulp of air. It worked like a drug, severing the tethers that tied her to reality.

"The silk would flow over your warm skin like water over marble."

His lips brushed her shoulder. She pushed her body up into his. Reflex. Her thoughts were delayed. As though out of sync with her body. All her body was concerned with was the heat in her belly, the fiery need that was eager to burn out of control.

"I'd fall to my knees before you." He was weaving a spell. Wrapping her up in the images in her head. Making reality fade. "My hands would curl into the hem at your ankles." His hand tucked under her T-shirt at her waist. Hot flesh found the small of her back, pressing her into him.

"I'd push the silk up your legs. Slowly, so slowly. Letting it glide over your hips. My lips would follow the trail, worshipping the skin it revealed, working to decide which was smoother, silk or skin." His teeth nipped at the cord in her neck. Her breathing was ragged. Her leg curled around his hip and denim scraped against her bare skin. The sensation made her need increase.

"Hot, enticing skin, wrapped in cool blue silk. A gift to unwrap. For me." He nibbled at her earlobe. Her heart was so loud it almost drowned out his words.

"My thumbs would press into the dips of your hips as my tongue drew slow circles on your stomach."

His lips nipped their way to her mouth. "I'd breath deep. Your desire would be unmistakeable. The scent of it would drive me wild. I'd have to fight to keep control." His tongue swept lazily across her bottom lip, and Magenta couldn't stifle a moan. He'd driven logical thought from her mind with his words. All that was left was her need. She wanted him. She had to have him. Now. Now. Now.

"I'd keep my control, Magenta," he whispered against her lips. "Do you know why?"

She didn't care. She couldn't get close enough to him. Her mind was spinning. Or maybe it was the room. Her mouth watered with the thought of tasting him. Her whole being was consumed with need. Desperate, hopeless need.

"I'd keep control because I wouldn't want to miss a second of touching you. I'd want to savour it. Prolong it. Commit each touch to memory. Until we were wrapped in each other. Only us. Moving together. Touching. Wanting. Needing. Nothing else. Only us."

"I can't stand it." Magenta's voice was a rasp. "Kiss me."

He smiled against her mouth before he did just that.

CHAPTER 12

She was wrapped around him. He felt the heat of her body pressed against his. Every shiver and tremble pushed his desire higher. Gods, but the taste of her. Ambrosia. Divine food of the gods. He knew there was nothing else on earth like it. He'd always known it would be like this. He'd been with other women, but he'd known, soul deep, that they had nothing on Magenta. No one did.

Her tiny whimper of need brought his thoughts back to her. Her slender hands moved to his hair, fingers weaving through it as she clung to him. She angled his head, kissing him deeper. Her passion ignited the dominant aspects of his nature that usually only surfaced during business or when he was fighting. It was important to him that he had control in this, for now. He wanted her to know that he wasn't a walkover. That she couldn't dismiss him easily. She couldn't frighten him away the way she did with anyone else who got too close. He was too strong for that.

He put a few scant inches between them as he grasped her hands. He wound their fingers together, holding her hands on the ground on either side of her head. "Not so fast, baby. I want you to enjoy this. Don't worry; I'll make you feel so good you'll have no problem relaxing for sleep."

Her body pushed up under him. "Talk. Talk. Talk. That's all I'm getting." She was annoyed. And breathless.

He grinned against her lips. "So demanding." He kissed her long and hard, stealing the breath from her. "I love it." Before she could answer, his mouth was back on hers.

Her body relaxed as tiny moans peppered the air. The sound made him almost rabid with want. She clenched his hands so hard he felt the bite of her nails. It made him growl. Almost loath to lose the nip of her touch, he transferred both of her hands into one of his and slid to her side. He was still pressed fully against her, her leg still over his hip, but now he could touch her. He wanted his hands on the curves he'd dreamed about.

She groaned her displeasure at losing his weight. It made him smile. His mouth found her neck, where he bit and sucked, noting which touch got the strongest reaction. Filing the information away for future use.

"Harry." It was barely a whisper, but it was filled with such longing it made his blood surge.

His hand skimmed over her shoulder, around the outer curve of her breast, over her hip to her thigh. She pressed into him, panting as his hand found skin. He held her tight at the curve where her thigh met her behind. His fingertips straying into the heat of her inner thigh. His lips moved to her ear.

"Do you want me to make you feel good? Do you want me to release the tension for you? I can. I can make your body do whatever I need it to do. Do you want that, Magenta?"

Her breath hitched. A gasp. "Harry."

"Tell me, baby, tell me you want me to touch you and make you lose control." His words were a dark mumble. Each one almost desperately tight.

"Harry?" He could hear the confusion. The need. She was somewhere else already. It made him want to roar with victory.

"Tell me," he ordered. "Tell me you want me to touch you."

He let his fingers whisper over her centre. Let her know exactly what he meant. She gasped and jolted into his touch.

"Harry. Please." The desperation he heard turned him inside out.

"Tell me." A whisper against her lips.

"Please touch me. Please make me soar."

He slumped against her. Relief flooding him. "My pleasure, baby. My pleasure." His mouth crashed on hers as his fingers slid under the cotton edge of her boy shorts. A second later, he found heaven. Wet. Ready. Pulsing with need.

His tongue plundered the depths of her mouth, while his nimble fingers teased her sensitive and needy core.

Her mewing sounds mingled with desperate pants. He caught each in his mouth. Savouring the taste of her desire. Swelling with pride at her loss of control.

"Please," she gasped. "Please."

He bit her full bottom lip, tugging it into his mouth. Her hands fought to be free. He pressed them into the earth, earning another moan. Her hips ground against his. Her calf clutched his hip. Her heel digging into his backside.

"I've got you," he told her. "Let go."

"Oh, oh, Harry!"

And then she was soaring, just like he'd promised she would. Harry covered her mouth with his to capture her moans. Feeling her buck beneath him. Holding her tight as her body spasmed and stretched. Gently, he coaxed her back down to earth. To him. His arms wrapped around her, as he fell to his back. He pulled Magenta on top of him.

With a kiss to her forehead, he stroked her hair.

"Harry," she said softly. She sounded dazed. Wrung out. Sated.

He smiled into her hair. "Sleep, baby. It'll soon be morning. Sleep here, with me."

"Harry, we need to—we should, I mean, there should be talking."

"Tomorrow. Tonight we sleep."

She lifted her head as though ready to protest.

"Please, baby, let me enjoy this. I've waited so long to be close to you. I don't want to miss a second. I want to hold you. I want you to sleep. Give me that."

She stilled for a moment, then her body relaxed. Slowly, she tucked her head back under his chin. Her hand snaked under his arm to curve up around him. Her knee bent to cuddle his hip. Harry held her close as her body went heavy with sleep. Her breathing deep and slow. He was never letting her go. Ever.

It was then he heard it, a whisper carried by the air. "Holy hell. Did you hear that? Harry has skills. Who knew? Is it wrong to get hot listening to your cousin get horizontal with your best friend? I might need therapy. And a man. I definitely need a man."

He'd forgotten that the people outside could hear them.

Harry's eyes clenched shut. His whole body became taut as he waited to see if Magenta had heard. When she didn't move and her steady breathing registered in his panicked mind, he allowed himself to relax.

There would be no sleep for him. He'd planned to spend his night memorising the feel of Magenta curled up against him. Instead he'd have to spend it thinking about what he would do in the morning. How he would deal with the fall-out. He needed a plan, because when that door opened and Magenta realised they'd had an audience, she was either going to kill him or hate him.

And he couldn't allow her to do either.

CHAPTER 13

Magenta couldn't look at Harry. She was mortified. She'd woken up wrapped around him, and her first thought had not been to run—no, her first thought had been that she should get him naked and lick him all over. Then she remembered they were in a tent. In a mine. And that she'd let him…hell, she couldn't even put into words what she'd let him do. Not that she didn't have the words. Just that she didn't want to use them in association with Harry.

She hung her head as she thought about it. Harry. The man she'd sworn to avoid. The man she'd made sure to get rid of when she was thirteen. The man she'd barely kissed before he'd had his hands in her knickers!

She was a slut. A big, stupid slut. She'd given it up for Harry in a dirty old mine. Not only that, but she'd begged him. And all of this after barely a kiss and not even one date.

She took a deep breath. Several, in fact. Okay. So the situation wasn't great. So getting physical with Harry hadn't been her best decision. It was still salvageable. It wasn't like anyone knew what they'd done. It wasn't like they'd gone on a date in public, where everyone in town would see and stick their noses in. She groaned. It wasn't like they'd gone on a date at all. Never mind that. It was a slip-up. A mistake. A lapse in control. And it wasn't like she planned to do it again. Oh, no. These were exceptional circumstances. Ones that would not be repeated. As soon as they got out of the mine, all she had to do was avoid him and make it clear that she had no interest in him.

Although how she'd manage that when she practically drooled every time he was near her, she didn't know. Flashes of the night before flitted through her mind. Her pulse sped up at the memories. She wanted to scream with frustration. She had to stop thinking about him like that. There was no future for them. She needed to go on a trip. Deep into the land of denial and avoidance, where she could enjoy a holiday from reality.

She eyed the door, which now had slivers of light shining around it like a beacon of hope. When were they going to open the door? Had Harry lied about it being this morning? No. Surely not. She checked her watch. Seven a.m. Too early for a rescue.

"You hungry?" Harry's voice jarred her out of her thoughts.

"Yes!" *Okay, dial it down a notch.* "I could eat." Hopefully the eating would fill the time until the rescuing. Oh, how she needed rescuing.

"What do you want? I've got…"

She held up a hand. "Please, don't list everything again. Give me a sandwich and a drink."

He gave her a lazy grin before passing her what she'd asked for.

"About last night…"

Magenta shot to her feet. "No about last night," she ordered. "No talking at all. Are we clear?"

"Baby." He cocked an eyebrow at her, with a look that

clearly said he thought she was overreacting. "We need to talk about last night. Then, once we have it sorted in your head, we need to repeat it. Soon. I'm thinking as soon as we get out of here. In a bed."

"Stop talking." She glared at him. "That's what caused this in the first place. You talk and then things happen. It's like some sort of voodoo or something. No. It's brainwashing. You brainwash me into doing your bidding with your sexy words. Lots and lots of sexy words. Aren't men supposed to be taciturn? I've known Lake for over a year and I'm sure he hasn't said more than ten words to me. Let's be like Lake. Let's not talk."

His smile turned dangerously sexy as he looked up at her through thick eyelashes. "You like it when I talk about sex? I can do that. I enjoy doing that."

"Are you even listening to me?" She was practically screeching, and she never screeched. Ever. "No talking. Stop it. Or I'm going to wait for the rescue in the mine." She folded her arms. "Alone."

He considered her for a minute. "You know, every time you fold your arms like that it presses your breasts together. Which makes me think of all the things I could do with them pressed together." His eyes went dark, which in turn made Magenta's mouth turn dry.

"That's it. I'm going into the mine. You can wait for the door to be opened on your own."

"Sit down." He rubbed a hand over his face. "I'll stop talking."

She stared at him for a moment, trying to gauge if he was telling the truth or not. Eventually, she relaxed and sat back down across from him, her back to the wall. They ate in silence.

"Morning, you two." Matt's voice was a welcome relief from the heaviness of *not* talking to Harry.

Magenta jumped up and ran to the door. "What's happening?"

"The council engineer is on his way up. He's going to pry the door open, jack the jamb in case it cracks and let you two out. Once he's done that, he'll check the entrance and secure the door." There was a pause. "Magenta, maybe you'd like to go back through the mine and come out the tunnel entrance in the hills?"

Magenta frowned in the direction Matt's voice came from. Harry shuffled his feet beside her.

"Why would I want to do that? I'll take two hours to get out that way, and your guy will have the door open long before then."

"Well…" Matt seemed stuck for words. "There's quite a crowd out here, and I know how you don't like being the centre of attention."

"He's got a point," Harry said. "You like being in the mine. It helps you relax. Maybe you should take an hour or two to do that before you head home."

She stared at Harry. His face was carefully blank. She moved to fold her arms, but remembered what Harry had said about that gesture. She put her hands on her jean-clad hips instead. "What's going on?"

"Yeah," Matt said. "Why don't you explain what's going on, Harry, while I deal with the engineer?"

Harry muttered something under his breath.

"Harry?" Magenta was losing patience.

He folded his arms, and she briefly wondered if she should point out that it made her want to bite his shoulder. She didn't, aware that would excite Harry, not irritate him, like his comment had irritated her. Sometimes the world wasn't fair.

"About last night…" Harry started.

Magenta held up her hands to stop him. "I told you, I don't want to talk about it."

"I understand that." Harry clenched his jaw. "But there are some aspects of last night that we need to talk about before we get out of here. Trust me."

"Not. Going. To. Happen." She turned her back on him.

"Magenta." Harry's frustration came through loud and clear.

Before he could say anything else, there was a loud rumble from outside the mine. "Stand well back from the door," someone shouted.

Magenta picked up her backpack and headed deeper into the mine. She'd wait by the tunnels. In the dark. Alone.

"Damn it," Harry muttered as he moved to follow her.

A few seconds later, she heard the welcoming sound of metal on metal as they started to pry open the door. Magenta couldn't wait to get out of the mine and away from Harry's magic fingers and sexy voice. Denial would be a lot easier to achieve if she didn't have him hanging around.

Magenta wouldn't talk to him. She wouldn't listen to him. And Harry knew from Matt's friendly suggestion that things were going to go to hell in a handbasket as soon as the door opened. He shook his head. There was nothing he could do except weather the oncoming storm. He couldn't even grab her to him and kiss some sense into her. She had on heavy climbing boots, and he valued his balls too much to try.

Harry had spent a wakeful night trying to figure out a solution to his problem. Even with his big brain, he'd come up with nothing. Nada. Zip. Nil. Nothing. His only option was to let this train wreck happen, then work at putting the pieces together afterwards. He watched Magenta out of the corner of his eye—assuming there were any pieces left.

Harry's back muscles became increasingly tight as the door began to open. Light flooded the room, to the point where it was almost blinding.

"About time," Magenta said.

Harry's jaw clenched. This was not going to be good.

The door opened far enough for a large machine to slip into the space. They heard a whirr as it stretched to fill the opening. It stopped when it was wedged tight between the floor of the mine and the jamb. Harry took a deep breath. This was it. Magenta swung her pack onto her back. Harry left his gear. He'd get it later. Slowly, the heavy door swung out—to a cheer.

"Mine rescues are always entertaining," Magenta told him.

He suspected that none of the previous ones had been as entertaining as this one.

"Okay, I'm off. Have a nice life, Harry." With that, Magenta stalked towards the open door.

With a sigh, Harry followed—and ran right into her back two steps outside the entrance. Magenta was a statue. He wasn't even sure she was breathing. She just stood there, transfixed by the raucous crowd in front of her. It seemed like most of Invertary was there to greet them. Harry spotted the knitting group—Knit or Die—who'd brought along picnic baskets, beach chairs and blankets. They were knitting while grinning in Magenta's direction.

"Good on you, girl," Jean shouted. "Don't let this one go. Any man who can make a girl scream like that is a man you hold on to."

The other women nodded their agreement.

Matt stood beside the door, dressed in full police gear, his arms folded and a scowl on his face. He caught Harry's eyes and gave him a look of disapproval. One Harry probably deserved.

"Go Harry, go Harry, go Harry." The twins started a chant, which drew his attention.

That was when he noticed they'd taken a black marker pen to their matching white T-shirts. They'd written: *Harry is a sex god.* Harry felt the blood drain from his face. This was not good.

"Harry," a guy from the back shouted. "You should run seminars. After last night, the missus was all over me."

"Aye," another guy yelled. "I need to write down some of those lines you used. Because they definitely worked."

Harry watched Magenta's shoulders straighten. A muscle on the side of her jaw twitched. Her backpack fell to the ground. Her hands went to her hips. She took a deep breath. *Here it comes*, Harry thought. *I'm dead.*

"Right, you bunch of perverts," Magenta shouted. "It's obvious you heard more than you should have. The show's over. It's time to go home."

Harry almost collapsed at her words. She wasn't embarrassed? He shot a look at Matt, who seemed equally stunned. Maybe this was part of the new, mature Magenta he hadn't met yet. She seemed to be taking the lack of privacy really well. Not at all like the old "hit first, ask questions later" Magenta he remembered from his childhood. Then it hit him. She'd assumed that being overheard was news to Harry too. She didn't realise he already knew they'd had an audience.

The crowd weren't pleased with her reaction. There were boos. Malcolm, the local newspaper editor, photographer and only journalist stuck a camera in their faces. "How about the two of you kiss? I could use a picture to go with this story, and one of you snogging is much better than a photo of the mine door. Not that it isn't a great door, but I'm sure you kissing will sell more papers."

"Not going to happen," Magenta said.

"Kiss Harry, kiss Harry, kiss Harry…" The twins changed their chant.

Magenta's cheeks began to flush pink, and for a moment Harry wondered if she was going to kiss him. Suddenly the day was perking up. He felt almost ashamed that he'd thought coming out of the mine would go badly. For one glorious moment, he thought he would get away with his scheming.

Then Betty pushed her way through the crowd. One look at the evil smile on her face and Harry saw his life flash before his eyes.

It all happened in slow motion. Betty opened her mouth as her eyes narrowed. Harry shouted "no" and lunged for Betty. Magenta stumbled to the side. The camera flashed. There was a shocked silence. Then Betty's voice rang out.

"Before you kiss him, you might want to know that you could have gotten out of the mine last night. Genius here paid off the engineer to wait till this morning."

Time stopped. The only sound was Betty's evil cackle.

Slowly, Magenta turned to Harry. Her eyes turned red and sparks flashed around her head.

"Harry?" Her voice was soft and deadly. "What's she talking about?"

"Oh crap, Harry's dead," someone in the crowd muttered.

They were not wrong.

"Harry?" Magenta's voice was tight.

Harry ran a hand through his hair. His big brain was blank. Bloody blank. Nothing. No excuses. No fabrications. No explanations. Nothing. He felt the crowd lean in towards them.

"I might have arranged for us to spend the night together."

The autumn air turned frigid.

"Did you know they could hear us?"

He leaned towards her and gave a small smile, hoping it might soothe her. It didn't. "Baby, I tried to get you alone. You were avoiding me. I was desperate."

His mistake was watching her eyes instead of her feet. Her eyes turned black. Her brow furrowed and then stars burst in Harry's vision. Pain shot through him. His knees crumpled beneath him and he writhed on the ground, unable to breathe, unable to do anything but whimper. His hands clutched his now, no doubt, pulverised balls. Too little, too late. Why hadn't he watched her feet?

Calmly, Magenta picked up her pack, stepped over him and started the long walk back to town.

"Somebody get ice," Matt shouted.

"I think I'm going to die." Harry strained to get the words out.

"You deserve to die, you bloody idiot," his cousin helpfully said.

An icepack was thrust at his groin.

"My work here is done," Betty said before trotting off down the hill.

A shadow covered Harry's face, and he looked up to find Rachel glaring down at him. "Can we go back to London *now*?" she said.

Harry closed his eyes and groaned.

CHAPTER 14

To say Magenta was angry would be like saying the Incredible Hulk had muscles. She was way past angry. She was livid. Furious. Murderous. And she knew exactly whom she wanted to kill. No, maim. Maybe torture first.

The twins fell into step beside her. Sandwiching her between them.

"Notice that we picked you over our cousin," Megan said.

"Even though he's no doubt lying there maimed, unable to father any children and crying for his mummy," Claire added helpfully.

Magenta rolled her eyes. "I didn't kick him full force. Just enough to make a point."

"Yeah, I'm sure he noticed the difference," Megan said.

"He deserved it."

There was silence. Magenta stopped on the rocky path, making her friends stop along with her.

"What?" she said. "You don't think he deserved that?"

They shared one of their telepathic looks, and Magenta felt her hackles rise.

"What we think is that he went to all that trouble to get

you alone. He was clearly worried about rats in there, but didn't let it stop him from spending time with you," Megan said.

"He gave you a superhot orgasm. Selflessly. We didn't hear him say, 'Hey, babe, now it's my turn,'" Claire said.

Magenta growled at them. They shared another look.

"We think it's kind of romantic," Megan said.

"Urgh!" Magenta stomped away from them, heading back down to town.

"Come on." Claire elbowed her. "You have to admit, it was kind of romantic. He went to all that trouble to get you alone, and then he took care of you." She paused. "As in *took care* of your sexual needs."

"I know what you meant," Magenta said through clenched teeth.

"I wish someone would do that for me," Megan said, sighing.

"Seriously? You wish a guy would lie to you to get you to spend the night with him, then let the town listen in while you get physical? Really? You think that would be super romantic? Pair of bubble heads."

"Hey," Claire said. "No name-calling."

"Fine. Sorry. I'm furious. And embarrassed. The whole town heard me. It's humiliating. I gave in to his charms. I fell for his tricks. Argh. I want to march back up there and kick him again."

"Honey." Claire threaded her arm through Magenta's, and Megan immediately did the same on the other side. Magenta suddenly felt like Dorothy on the yellow brick road. All she needed was some skipping and singing. And a yappy, annoying dog. No, wait. Betty was behind them. They had yappy and annoying covered.

"You don't want to waste precious time and energy being angry," Megan said.

"Yes, I do. I really, really do," Magenta told them. Because as soon as the anger calmed down, she'd have to deal with the humiliation, and that was *not* something she was looking forward to.

"No, you don't. What you need to do is get even." Claire grinned. "When we were kids and the boys did something that was mean or embarrassing to us, we'd hit them harder. They soon learned that they couldn't mess with the girls. You need to teach this lesson to Harry. Sure, he was sexy and unselfish in the mine, and it was kind of romantic—although I can totally see why you don't think so. I do get that he manipulated you and then publically humiliated you. What you need to do is repay that favour. A swift kick is great, but you aren't thinking big enough."

"Or being creative enough," Megan added.

"Don't worry," Claire said. "We'll help you turn this situation on its head so that people won't be talking about the time Harry conned Magenta into getting naked in the mine. No, they'll be talking about what Magenta did to Harry afterwards."

"He'll be a lesson to all the men of Invertary," Megan said.

"Yes," Claire said. "You can't mess with the women of this town."

Magenta found herself smiling at the twins. They were right. She shouldn't get mad. She should get even.

"I'm in." She was relieved to find the embarrassment wasn't as overwhelming now she had a plan.

Harry was going to seriously regret messing with Magenta.

CHAPTER 15

"Have you seen this?" Rachel slammed the paper down in front of Harry.

He was perched on a chair at the table in Lake's office, wishing he still had a bag of frozen peas wedged against his crotch. It had been two days since the mine incident, but he still ached. "Black and blue" did not cover it. Thankfully, everything was still in working order. He knew because thinking about Magenta still had the same effect it'd always had. Seemed there was nothing that woman could do to put him off.

He looked at the front page of the *Invertary Standard*. There he was, lying on the ground writhing in pain while Magenta glared down at him. The heading said: *Mayhem at Magenta's Mine.*

"That's a rubbish headline," Harry said. "It doesn't tell you anything about the story under it."

Rachel glared at him, so he smiled sweetly. It had no effect.

"'Millionaire programming genius Harry Boyle,'" Rachel

read, "'bit off more than he could chew this week when he conned his current crush into spending a night with him in the local mine. Unfortunately for the pair, the mine acts like an echo chamber, making it easy for the town to hear every word, gasp and moan they made during their night together. Magenta Fraser did not take the news of the town witnessing their liaison well. After kicking Harry in the groin, she stormed off, leaving their relationship in the dust, along with her man. She has been unavailable for comment.'"

Rachel slapped the paper down. "It goes on to say that the town's men are taking notes on your seduction technique because you talked your way into Magenta's knickers in record time."

Was it wrong he felt proud? Probably.

"This has gone viral on the web. Someone shot footage of the spat and put it on YouTube. It's going to affect business."

"I don't see how," Harry said. "Most of people we deal with are geeks. They can't get near a woman. This will impress them."

Rachel smacked him on the back of his head.

"We also deal with the government. Lots of governments. Do you think this makes you look mature? Respectable? Reliable? We deal with people who don't like attention, and you're on YouTube." She folded her arms over a form-fitting black suit. "Now do you see how it affects business?"

"Fine. You're the business guru, tell me how we sort this."

She fixed him with a glare. "We move back to London, you wear a suit, you keep your head down and we quietly take meetings where you act like a grown-up."

He shook his head. "I don't want to go back to London. I want to close the deal on the office space we found here. I need to stay in Invertary. I need to sort this out with Magenta."

She slapped the table in front of her. "Are you out of your freaking mind? The girl doesn't want anything to do with you. Most men who get kicked in the balls figure that out for themselves."

"Nuh-uh, she's interested. You weren't in there with us. Trust me, she's interested. I just need to figure out what's holding her back. There has to be something."

"For the love of all things chocolate," Rachel wailed. "Listen to yourself. You're screwing up the business we worked hard to build so you can chase a woman who does not want you." She turned to Lake, who had been sitting silently at his desk through all of this. "Tell him, will you?"

Lake stared at Harry for a minute. Harry almost squirmed. He could believe Lake used to be an interrogation specialist.

"You want her. Get her," Lake said.

Harry grinned. Rachel threw up her hands in disgust. "I'm surrounded by cavemen. Is it the effect of the Highlands? Does everyone who comes up here get the urge to go all Braveheart? Is that what this is?"

"*You can take my life, but you can never take my freedom,*" Harry said solemnly.

"I give up. I need chocolate." With that, Rachel stormed out of the room.

Harry turned to Lake. "Any ideas on how to fix this?"

"Well, for one, I wouldn't take any more advice from Betty."

Yeah, Harry had already figured that part out for himself. "Anything else?"

"Man up. Don't retreat. Be strategic. Strategy wins the war."

"Okay," Harry said slowly. He had no idea what any of that meant.

Lake grunted and went back to work.

. . .

"I'M NOT sure I like this plan," Magenta said.

"This plan is awesome," Claire told her.

"Harry's going to freak out."

"That's why it's awesome."

"We could traumatise him for life." Although she'd been avoiding Harry in the week since the mine moaning incident —as the twins were calling it—she still wasn't sure she wanted him to suffer. Her anger had worn off, and she was left feeling oddly protective of the man. Even though he was the reason for the stream of people who'd come through the shop purely to gawk at her. "He really seems to have some sort of phobia. I'm not sure this is the best way to get back at him. We should think of something else."

"Stop being a big chicken." Megan dragged the last two bags from the car.

Magenta straightened her shoulders. Megan was right. She was being pathetic. The fallout from Harry's trickery would last for months. Long after he got fed up with Invertary and crawled back to London.

She ignored the part of her that balked at the thought of upsetting Harry, and narrowed her eyes. "Let's get to it."

"That's the spirit." Claire pulled out a key to her brother's police-issue house and opened the door. "Had to steal the key from Mum. Matt won't let us have a key because he doesn't trust us."

"Because he thinks we're still ten years old and up to no good." Megan rolled her eyes.

Magenta gaped at them. "You *are* up to no good, you pair of bubble heads."

"Name-calling, Magenta—remember we talked about that." Megan smothered a giggle as Claire used her kindergarten teacher voice.

They let themselves into Matt's house, which was a standard 1970s box with no personality whatsoever. It even had orange glass in half the windows. Magenta shuddered. Inside it was pristine. So much so that she wondered if Matt actually lived there.

"Harry's staying in the spare room," Claire told them as they made their way up the stairs. The twins were carrying several large bags and Magenta was carrying a cage.

"Here it is." Megan threw open the door at the end of the short hallway.

The room was pin neat, like the rest of the house.

"Are we sure he's staying here?"

Megan opened the closet and pulled out a T-shirt with Einstein's head on it. "Yep, this is his room."

"Okay." Magenta took a deep breath. "I guess we better get on with it, then."

The twins upended the bags they'd carried from the car and about a hundred toy rats fell out. They giggled as they threw them around the room.

"Unscrew the overhead light," Claire ordered. "That way he'll have to walk into the room to put the lamp on."

Megan pulled a chair over from the desk and removed the light bulb. "You got the camera?" she said to her sister.

Claire dug around in the messenger bag that was slung across her body and came out with a webcam. She stuck it above the door, facing the room. A minute later, she dug out her iPad and connected to the camera. "Perfect. We can see most of the room." She pointed at the camera. "Motion and sound sensors. It will activate when Harry comes in the room." She grinned widely. "Our cousin isn't the only one with mad computer skills." The twins high-fived with glee.

"Hold on a minute," Magenta said. "Where did you get the camera?"

"Lake's security shop," Megan said.

Magenta smacked her palm to her forehead. "Then Harry knows all about this."

Claire rolled her eyes. "Do we look stupid? We waited until Betty was manning the shop and bought it then."

"Yeah, let's trust Betty. That always goes well," Magenta said.

The twins ignored her. Instead they spent a few minutes arranging the rats around the room to make them look more realistic. They seemed pleased with the result. Magenta had to admit: in the dim light, the toys looked pretty real.

"Your turn," Claire told Magenta.

Magenta walked to the bed carrying the cage. She pulled two balls of tightly wrapped fat, seeds and meat from a plastic bag in her pocket. She put one on top of the bed covers and one under the covers. "Here goes nothing," she muttered as she opened the cage.

Three large rats, straight from a pet store in Fort William, ran for the ball of food.

"Quick. Out of the room," Megan said. "We don't want them to escape."

The girls ran for the door, slammed it shut behind them and sprinted down the stairs. Only when they were far away from Matt's house did they stop to talk.

"Do you think anyone saw us?" Claire was wide-eyed with worry.

"Does it really matter?" Magenta said. "As soon as they see what's in there, they'll know it's us."

"Good point," Claire said.

Megan linked her arms with her friend and sister. "I guess all we can do now is find a spot to watch and wait."

"You're sure he's coming home after seeing Lake?" Magenta uncharacteristically gnawed her lip.

"Yep, he arranged to meet Matt there. I heard them set it up."

Magenta let out a breath.

"Pub for dinner?" Claire said.

There was a nod of agreement. Still holding each other, the girls headed the short distance to the high street and Invertary's only pub.

CHAPTER 16

"Let me get changed," Harry shouted to his cousin as he entered the house. "Then we can go get something to eat."

"Why bother? You're only going to swap one inane T-shirt for another."

Harry ignored Matt, who was watching CNN on the widescreen in the living room. He didn't have time to deal with him. His hands were full coping with Magenta. He'd left her alone long enough to calm down. She got one more night. Then he planned to hunt her down and make her talk to him. Even if it meant tying her to a chair to do it. Or the bed. Mmm, yeah, tying her to the bed was a way better idea.

He swung open his room door and flicked on the light. Darkness prevailed. "Bring me a light bulb, will you?" he shouted to Matt. "The one in my room has blown."

He heard grumbling, but assumed Matt was digging out a bulb.

His mind on Magenta, Harry strode into the room, reached for the bedside lamp and was about to press the switch when he heard it. Scraping. Gnawing. His hand stilled. His body froze. Slowly, he turned his head towards the bed. Something moved. His heart shot to his mouth. Moving nothing but his finger, Harry switched on the lamp. The blood drained from his body.

Sitting in the middle of his bed was a huge white rat. It stopped nibbling on whatever the hell it was nibbling on, and its beady pink eyes stared at Harry. Evil eyes. Red like the devil. Harry couldn't breathe. Couldn't move. Couldn't think. Then he saw movement under his duvet. He sucked in a breath. His eyes shot to his pillow, where yet another tail twitched. His heart stopped beating altogether. He caught sight of something on the floor. His eyes flicked to it. Huge grey rats, under the furniture, peeking out from behind the chair. His heart restarted. His feet shuffled towards the door. He felt something squish under them, and looked down to see a rat's tail poking out from beside his boot.

And then he did what every man in the same situation would have done. He screamed like a baby, while throwing himself in the direction of the door. A doorway Matt had just appeared in, looking dumbfounded and carrying a light bulb.

"What the hell?" Matt said as Harry pushed him out of the way.

He tripped over his cousin to land on his knees in the hall.

"Rats!" He was beyond caring that he was hysterical, shouting his lungs out. "Rats in my room. Rats!" He stopped shouting and started to rant. "Shut the door. Lock the door. Don't go in there. I'll call the rat guy. We'll kill them all. Hairy little freakoids with their Satan-red eyes and germ-carrying teeth."

Matt shook his head and stepped into the room.

"Don't do it." Harry lunged at him. "They'll get you."

It was too late. He'd lost his cousin. He stumbled to his feet, fully intending to lock Matt in there, along with the rats, until the exterminator got there. It was too late to save his cousin now.

"Catch," Matt shouted, and something came flying at Harry.

He saw the grey hair first and just about passed out. Without thinking, he actually caught the damn thing. A rat. A squishy, soft rat. A velvet rat? A rat with no bones? A rat that didn't move? He looked down at the creature in his hands and felt his world tilt.

"I'm going to kill her," he said through gritted teeth.

Matt was laughing too hard to reply. Harry's heartbeat settled into a normal rhythm, and anger replaced panic.

"You are such a loser." Matt leaned against the doorframe, his laughter now reduced to an oversized grin. "The twins got you with something almost identical to this when you were a kid."

Where exactly did his cousin think his fear of rats came from?

He noticed something moving at his mocking cousin's feet. The white rat. Harry couldn't speak. He pointed.

"Rat," Harry said. "Real rat."

"Yeah, right." Matt looked down. The laughter stopped. His cousin let out a stream of curses as he paled. With lighting reflexes, Matt kicked the rat back into the room and slammed the door shut.

They stood side by side, shaking as they studied the door.

Harry pointed at the bottom of the door. "Rats can squeeze through spaces smaller than that gap."

Matt's face was thunderous when he stomped into the bathroom and came back with two towels. He rolled them up and wedged them under the door. They stared at it. Without talking, Matt left again, disappearing into his room. Harry stared at his bedroom door while listening as Matt dismantled something. A minute later, his cousin appeared with a long shelf and several hand weights. He placed the shelf against the towels and then wedged the weights up against it.

"They won't get through that." He didn't sound pleased. He sounded grim. Matt turned to Harry. "I'm going to kill them."

Harry nodded. It was obvious Matt wasn't talking about the rats. "You deal with your sisters. I'll handle Magenta."

Matt's eyes darkened as he nodded. "First I need to call pest control." He shuddered before stomping down the stairs.

Harry followed, taking the toy rat with him.

IN A BOOTH IN THE PUB, the twins and Magenta were laughing so hard that they had to hold each other upright. They weren't the only ones. Dougal had talked them into plugging Claire's iPad into the TV over the bar. Everyone got to watch, and listen, to the Harry and Matt show. Magenta had gotten over her anxiety about the plan and thought it was only fair that everyone watched. After all, the whole town had listened in on the mine debacle too.

"That was priceless." Dougal wiped tears from his eyes.

"I don't know what they were doing out in the hall," Josh McInnes said. "Maybe building a barricade. Wish I could have seen it." He turned to the girls. "Next time, two cameras."

Considering the American singer was one of Matt's best friends, Magenta was surprised he'd enjoyed the show so much.

"The way Matt lobbed the rat onto the bed with his boot." Josh's manager and best friend said. "Fantastic. The damn rat didn't even blink; it just turned around and started eating again."

"You can't let them kill the pet rats," one of the ladies of Knit or Die said. "That's plain wrong."

Claire shook her head. "I'm not going anywhere near Matt or Harry. Someone else will have to rescue the rats."

"I second that," Megan said.

Everyone turned to Magenta. "Don't look at me. I'd have to be nuts to go near those two right now."

"I'll deal with the rats," Lake said from beside Josh.

The girls beamed at him. "Our hero," Claire told him, making his lip twitch.

"In the meantime." Dougal's booming voice filled the room. "You girls better find a good hiding place. Those boys are going to be out for blood."

"Like it's something we aren't used to." Megan snorted. "We've been at war with them since we were born." She looked around the bar. "In case anyone is interested, the girls are winning."

There was a cheer. Once people turned their attention back to their food and each other, Magenta leaned in towards the twins. She kept her voice low so that Lake, Josh and Mitch couldn't hear them and tell tales to Matt. "I'm taking off for the mine for a few days until this calms down. It's the one place Harry won't look for me."

"Good thinking," Claire said. "We're going to spend some time with our parents. Matt won't do anything there."

"Well, he can try, but Mum will lecture him for about a year," Megan said. "He's ten years older than us; he's supposed to look out for us." She beamed. "It's my favourite lecture. Matt glowers, but he's immobilised."

"Okay, let's head back to the house and pick up our gear before the boys hunt us down." Magenta stood and tugged down her black leather mini-dress. It had silver studs around the neckline and a silver chain around the waist. With her thigh-high black leather platform boots and fishnet tights, she was going for a dominatrix-like don't-mess-with-me vibe. So far, so good.

"That was brilliant," Megan said on a sigh. "It's been years since we pulled a prank on Harry. I miss this."

"Me too," said Claire. "Being mature can really suck sometimes."

Magenta bit back a laugh. She didn't think the twins had to worry. They, along with her, were in no danger of being called mature any time soon.

CHAPTER 17

The three women charged up the path that led to the old terraced house they shared. The house was small: two bedrooms and a bath upstairs, living room and dining kitchen downstairs. The reason it worked for the three of them was that the owners had added a conservatory to the back of the house. They used that space as their living room, and Magenta claimed the room at the front of the house as her bedroom. That left one bedroom each for the twins, which was perfect, because no one would survive if they had to share a room.

The twins ran for the stairs. "Meet you back here in a minute," Claire called over her shoulder.

"I need to get changed and grab my gear pack. Won't be long." Magenta threw open the door to her room and strode to her wardrobe. She had her dress halfway over her head when the door slammed. Squealing, she pulled the dress back down and spun towards the noise. Harry was leaning against her door.

His arms were crossed over his chest and his ankles were lazily crossed in front of him. If it wasn't for the determination in his eyes, she would have thought he was perfectly happy to be there.

"Freaking hell, Harry, you've turned into a Peeping Tom now?"

"To be a Peeping Tom, I'd have to hide. Do I look like I'm hiding?" He spread his arms wide.

No. He was taking up far too much space to be anything but very, very visible. The sight of him in her room was enough to distract Magenta from her normal reaction—anger. She had to resort to faking it.

"What are you doing here?" she snapped, and hoped it sounded genuine.

"You spent time in my room. Only fair I get to spend time in yours." He reached into his back pocket, pulled something out and threw it at her. "Fido wanted his mummy."

She caught the toy rat. Against her better judgment, a smile fought to escape. "Fido?"

He shuddered. "Better than Plaguemeister."

A ruckus in the hall snatched Magenta's attention away from Harry.

"You can't do this," one of the twins shouted.

"Breaking and entering. Vandalising a police officer's house. Stealing a key from our mother. Attempted murder." Matt's voice was steel.

"Attempted murder?" someone screeched.

"You tried to kill Harry. He damn near had a heart attack."

"No he didn't. We watched the whole thing in the pub. There was no heart attack, but he did nearly pee his pants."

The idiots giggled. Even Magenta rolled her eyes.

"Ow, let go, Don Don."

"No. You two are going to spend the night in a nice cold cell. Might give you some time to consider a change in behaviour."

"You can't do this. I want a lawyer. I want my phone call."

Matt laughed. "So you can call Mum and I can spend the night listening to her go on about how precious my baby sisters are? Nuh-uh, not going to happen. Come on, dumb and dumber. If you're really good I won't put the rats in the cell with you. The live ones. Not the toys."

The voices faded as the twins shouted at Matt all the way to his police car. Magenta looked at Harry. "He can't do that, can he?"

"Who's going to stop him?"

He had a point. As they said in those old western movies —Matt was the law around these parts.

Magenta put her hands on her hips and glared at Harry, pleased to feel some of her irritation return. Obviously not all of her common sense was derailed purely by Harry's presence. "So, genius, do you have a plan or are you going to stand there and stare at me all evening?"

She heard the lock turn before Harry pushed away from the door. The look in his eye was intense, focused and sent shivers she didn't want to experience running down her spine.

"I have a plan. You're going to get changed into your nightwear. I'm going to kick off my shoes and then we are going to climb into that bed and..." He stood in front of her, close enough to touch. "Talk. We're going to talk." He cocked an eyebrow at her. "It's long overdue, don't you think?"

Magenta retreated. Being around Harry clouded her brain. She needed some space to think. She walked over to the window, where a small settee sat, deliberately keeping her eyes off her queen-sized bed. The image of Harry and a bed in her head at the same time wasn't good for her sanity.

"I don't want to talk. I don't want you here. I don't want to have anything to do with you."

He actually laughed. As in hard enough to double over

and hold his knees. "That's priceless. You want me so bad you can hardly think."

"Wow, arrogant much?"

"Accurate much. You've wanted me for years." The smug look on his face made her fingers curl into fists.

"I have not."

He gave her a wicked smile. "I found proof. I found the scrapbook."

Her world tilted. Her eyes shot to the bottom drawer of the Scotch chest where she kept things that were important to her—like a scrapbook full of news about Harry. Photos from their shared childhood. Pictures of his graduation that his mother had sent her, and the invitation to attend that Magenta had ignored. A pressed flower, a gift during a walk when she was twelve and Harry was messing around, calling her princess. Tickets from movies they'd seen together. Newspaper articles about his company and how brilliant he was. Everything that had anything to do with Harry was in there—right back to the very first Christmas card he'd given her when she was five. Even the black-and-white photo of him she'd kissed wearing pink lip gloss when she was twelve, thinking it was a romantic thing to do. Now the thought made her want to vomit.

She closed her eyes for a second as humiliation swept over her. He'd have seen the doodles she did when she was thirteen and he was away at university. She'd missed him so much and spent her time writing his name all over her books. Along with curly, girly repetitions of her wished-for future married name—Maggie Boyle. She took a deep breath. It was fine. It was all fine. None of it meant anything. She'd been a kid. She wasn't a kid anymore.

"You are way out of line, nosing around in my private belongings like that. I don't care what you think you saw.

That stuff doesn't matter anymore. I only keep it for sentimental reasons."

Harry gave her a look that said, *Yeah, right.* He turned, grabbed a chair from her desk, plonked it in front of the door and sat in it. "Tell yourself whatever you like, but I know the real reason I rate a whole book full of mementoes."

Magenta took a deep breath. She was about five seconds away from wiping that superior smile off his face.

"What would that be, Harry? Do enlighten me."

His wide, wicked grin made her wobble.

"You're in love with me."

Her world stopped for a second before it resumed spinning again.

"In your dreams." Damn, why did she sound so shaky? Why wasn't she denying his claim? Her palms were clammy and her brain was fuzzy. It had to be Harry's pheromones attacking her hormones, making her lose her mind to lust. Not love. Lust. It didn't sound convincing even to her.

"No, baby, in *your* dreams, but I can make it reality. You love me, and here I am." He spread his arms wide. "Here for the taking."

She didn't know whether to laugh or gag at the cheesiness of it all. Undecided, she folded her arms.

"I think it's time you went home," she told him.

"I would, but my room is full of rats. I can't go back there. Ever. Guess you have a new roomie."

"Over your dead body."

"I'd rather be alive. If I'm sharing your bed, I'd like to enjoy the experience."

"You can't stay here."

"My bed is full of rats. Your bed is full of you. It doesn't take a rocket scientist to make the right choice."

"I don't want you here."

"Yes, you do." He looked so damn smug that it made her

fists itch to strike out. "You want me here because you love me."

"Argh!" She stomped over to the window as she fought the urge to scream loudly.

"Don't even think about trying to get out through the windows," Harry said. "I spent time jamming them when I first got here."

She eyed her mobile phone, which was sitting on the desk.

"Who you gonna call? Ghostbusters?" He grinned, like this was the best entertainment he'd ever had. "That's about your only option, seeing as the sole cop within miles is busy locking up your roommates."

Man, sometimes it seriously sucked to live in a small town.

"Fine," she ground through a clenched jaw. "We can talk. What do you want to talk about?"

His eyes narrowed. "Change first. There's no way you want to sleep in that."

"I said we can talk. I didn't say we had to be in bed to do it."

"We're talking in bed. Where I can make sure you don't run. Where I can hold you while we talk about some heavy stuff. So get changed, or go to bed dressed as a dominatrix. It's up to you. But that doesn't look comfortable to sleep in."

HARRY WATCHED as each of Magenta's emotions worked their way across her face. Anger. Anxiety. Lust. Longing. Fear. Pain. Anger again. Oh yeah, *lots* of anger. He made sure to guard his crotch while he watched her think. She was a spitfire, one that could go off in his direction at any minute. She was also sexy as hell in the head-to-toe leather she was sporting. Some guys he knew had a leather fetish. They dreamed of women in leather. Harry had always thought it stemmed from too much time watching *Xena: Warrior Princess* in their formative years. Seeing Magenta in her form-fitting dress that looked as smooth as butter, he changed his opinion. Leather—good. He almost purred at the sight. Leather *really* good.

"Stop looking at me like that, you perv." Magenta placed her hands on her hips and scowled. It only enhanced the dominatrix vibe.

"I like the leather look on you." He caught her eyes, daring her to look away. "I like any look on you."

Her cheeks flushed and she licked her lips. He liked that. A lot.

"You've got two minutes to get changed, then we go to bed with you dressed like that."

She didn't move a muscle. Harry could have sworn she was trying to pierce holes through his skull with her eyes. Cute.

"Okay, time's up." He lazily stood, noticing that Magenta tensed. She was going to attack. That was *not* going to happen.

As quick as lightning, he bent over, thrust a shoulder in her stomach and scooped her up. Ten seconds later, he dumped a cursing Magenta in the middle of her bed and landed beside her. He rolled her to her side as she kicked and shouted. He wrapped an arm around her, pinning her arms to her sides and holding her tight, at the same time throwing a heavy leg over hers. She was immobilised, her back tucked tight against his front. He nuzzled her neck, knowing full well if he put any distance between their heads she'd use hers as a weapon. And Harry was fond of his nose the way it was.

"I am going to hurt you," Magenta said. The words vibrated with anger. "As soon as I'm free, you are going to be in so much pain."

"Better make sure I never let you go, then." He kissed her neck, making her growl in frustration.

"If you think this is the way to get me to talk, then you're insane. The last thing I want to do is have a heart-to-heart with you. You can hold me here all you like, Harry, but we are not talking."

"Fine, we'll snuggle instead." He wriggled closer to her, feeling her tense even more. "I like snuggling. I can snuggle all night."

They lay like that, in silence, Harry listening to Magenta huff and puff in annoyance, while the sun disappeared and darkness filled the sky. Magenta's bedroom was bathed in shadows. Harry hoped the darkness would work in his favour, the way it had in the mine.

Hours passed as he waited for the most stubborn woman he'd ever met to let go of her anger. It was a long wait. At last he felt her body relax against him. He gave it another few minutes before he spoke.

"Why did you cut me out of your life when you were thirteen, Magenta?" His voice was soft and intimate. A whisper between lovers.

The tension surged back into her body as the question registered.

"I don't want to talk about it." Her tone was without inflection. It was as though she bit out the words.

"I need to know. I've been trying to talk to you for years. Every time I came back for a visit, I'd make an effort to see you and you always shut it down. This time I'm back for good, I'm not going away and you can't ignore this thing between us."

She growled, but didn't deny his claim. It gave Harry hope. He caressed her hair with his nose, breathing in the scent that was purely Magenta. He didn't know what the fragrance was, if he got the chance he'd raid the bathroom so he could find out. Right now, he loved that the scent was unique to her.

"Everything was fine until I went to uni," he said softly. "I remember talking to you about it before I left. You knew how worried I was, scared to be starting uni when I wasn't even sixteen. You told me not to worry. You told me that, no matter what, I'd come back to Invertary and you'd be there for me." He took a deep breath and shook off the old pain of rejection. He was an adult. There was no room in his life for the anxieties of his childhood. He'd been devastated for a time, a long time. Eventually he'd come to realise that Magenta had a reason for what she did. Now he wanted to know what it was. It was the only way they could get past it and move on to the type of relationship he knew they were meant to have.

"I came home after the first term and you'd changed," he said. "Your hair was black, your clothes were black. It was as though someone had sucked the colour out of you. I remember the pain in your eyes even though you were sneering at me at the time. I remember the words—*You're a freak. A loser geek, Hairy Boil. I was embarrassed hanging out with you, and now that you aren't here I don't have to pretend I like you anymore. I only pretended to be your friend because I felt sorry for you. Now you can make new loser geek friends in uni and I can hang out with normal people. Go back to Glasgow, where you belong.*"

Magenta sucked in a breath. He heard the pain in it and knew he'd been right in thinking that saying those words had hurt her as much as hearing them had hurt him.

"I was devastated," Harry whispered. "But I got over it. It took me about a year. Eventually I started thinking with my head and not my broken heart. You were the one person in the world who knew me well enough to know exactly where to hit to get me to back off. You used every one of my insecurities to get me to leave you. It took me a while to figure it out. To realise that there was pain in your eyes. To realise that you didn't mean what you said."

Magenta trembled against him. He held her tightly. "It's okay. Really. The words don't mean anything to me now. They don't hurt or bother me. I'm not a kid anymore. I'm an adult. The only thing that bothers me now is why you said that to me. I want to know why you pushed me away. I want us to move past this." He took a deep breath. "You need to tell me why you did it."

The silence was deafening. It lasted so long that Harry was beginning to fear that she would never talk. That they would never be able to bridge the chasm between them. That she was lost to him forever.

Magenta cleared her throat. Harry dared hope. He stared into the warm shadows, made by the glow of the orange streetlights outside, and waited.

"You are so smart," she whispered. "Like, Stephen Hawking smart."

She fell silent. He loosened his grip, enabling him to caress her arm, hoping that each gentle touch would reassure her enough to get her talking again. He wanted to tell her that he wouldn't judge. That he wouldn't hate her. He hoped she got the message from the way he touched her. He hoped she felt exactly how precious she was to him.

"I'm not smart," she said at last in a small voice that broke his heart.

Although his need to refute her claim was strong, he didn't say anything. He suspected she needed the silence to continue talking. Instead of verbal reassurance, he kissed her neck and held her tightly.

She took a shaky breath. "I mean, I'm *really* not smart. I made it through primary school, although I spent a lot of time in remedial lessons."

Harry stilled, wondering how he could have missed that. But then, their time in primary school had been all about play, not what was happening in class.

"When I hit high school, things got worse. I couldn't keep up with anything." She let out a deep, shuddering breath. "I can't read properly, Harry. I can't write properly. The kids in school thought it was hilarious. They called it baby writing."

Harry closed his eyes and nuzzled her hair. The pain he felt for her was overwhelming.

"That first year in secondary school, when I was twelve and you were still there, was a shock. I failed at everything. I could understand the teachers fine when they were talking about the subjects, but as soon as I had to read or write anything, it became a mess. I did better in the practical subjects, like art and gym, but even then, when we had to write notes or read up on something, I screwed up." Her voice hitched. "The kids called me Maggie the moron. They would throw things at my head in class when the teacher wasn't looking. They stole my books because they said I didn't need them. *What's an idiot like you doing with books, Maggie? You're too thick to read them.*"

Harry wished he could turn back time and make those kids pay. He didn't ask why Magenta hadn't told him at the time. He knew why: he'd been an outcast too because of his big brain and because he'd been applying to uni while most kids his age were struggling with basic algebra. They'd both had to deal with their share of cruel jibes and rude comments. The difference was that Harry also got a lot of respect because he was so bright. Magenta hadn't had that.

"There was a teacher—Mrs. Adams, remember her?" Magenta sounded wistful.

He had to clear his throat because of the emotion blocking it. "English teacher. Young and pretty."

"Yeah, that's the one. She wanted me to be assessed. I

don't know what kind of assessment she meant, but the thought of it scared me. Mum went up to the school, and you know what she's like."

Harry grunted. Magenta's mother did whatever she could to be the centre of attention. If that meant stopping her daughter from getting the help she needed, she'd do exactly that.

"Anyway, Mrs. Adams spoke to Mum about getting me assessed, and Mum refused outright. She said that I was fine the way I was. She told her that not everyone could be as clever as my sister Grace. She said they were putting too much pressure on me, expecting too much. Mum told me later that she was worried they'd take me away from her and put me in a special school. She'd heard about a school in Glasgow where all the stupid kids went. She was worried I'd be locked up with them."

Harry clenched his jaw at the thought of Magenta's mum's wilful ignorance. "You know there isn't a school like that, right? Your mum's imagination got the better of her."

"I know that now," she said, although she didn't sound convinced. "Back then I was worried I'd be sent away because I was too stupid for school."

"You're not stupid, Magenta, don't say that."

There was silence. Harry petted Magenta to soothe her, and hoped it helped.

"While you were gone at uni, things got worse. Everywhere I turned, people were telling me I was dumb. The kids at school. The teachers who tried to push me. My mum, who kept reassuring me that it was okay to be stupid. That she was happy that I would never want to leave her and go to college, like Grace did." She scoffed. "Mum's reassurance was a lot like other people's bullying." She sighed at the memory, and Harry clenched his jaw with the need to have a little talk with her mother.

"I knew I had to do something to defend myself," Magenta said. "I had to learn how to care less about the fact I was so thick. I had to stop being a target for everyone. So I changed. I became Magenta. Magenta skipped school and flipped off the teachers when they tried to push her too hard. Magenta punched the kids who called her names. Magenta disrupted the classes she couldn't cope with. I was particularly bad in English class, which made Mrs. Adams sad. I still see the tears in her eyes. I hated that look. I hated her for pitying me."

"Maybe she was worried about you, baby."

"Maybe."

"When you came back after your first term at university, I couldn't let you know how dumb I was. I wanted you to think well of me. I wanted you to think I was normal. I couldn't stand the thought that you might look at me the way the other kids did, like I was nothing. If the normal kids noticed how stupid I was and thought less of me, then how would someone as smart as you feel about it? I couldn't take the chance that you would reject me. It would have broken me. So I rejected you first." She took a deep breath. "It was the right thing to do. We're worlds apart. You're a genius with a business that earns millions. You can hold your own with governments, academics and security specialists. You're smart, kind, funny and confident. And you can kick ass with the best of them.

"I work in a lingerie shop. I never finished school. I don't have an email account, or text people, because I can't read and write properly. I've never read a book all the way through because the words jump around and it takes me a day to read a page. I struggle reading maps, signs and instructions on medication. I'm not funny, kind or confident. I pretend to be. Mostly I'm just prickly. I know, deep inside, with an unshakeable certainty, that I am not as clever as the people around me and that I'll be ashamed when they find out. All of my energy goes into hiding who I really am—the stupid girl. The one that can't even fill in a form. Even the twins don't know how dumb I am."

She wriggled in his arms and Harry let her turn. She lay on her back beside him, looking up at him. "You understand, don't you? A relationship between us would never work. You would get bored being with someone like me. You'd get frustrated because I couldn't keep up with you intellectually, or you'll become embarrassed because I can't do the basic stuff other people can do. Do you see why I told you to leave me alone all those years ago? Do you understand why nothing has changed?" She shook her head. "No, some things have changed. You're even smarter, and now you're sexy and respected too. But I'm still the same. I'm still here. In town. Wearing black and cheesing people off. You need to go back to London where you belong." She gave him a tremulous smile. "And please take Executive Barbie with you. The town isn't ready for her."

Harry attempted a smile at her joke about Rachel. He gently brushed her hair back from her face, then caressed her cheek. It would be so easy to fall into those wide honey eyes of hers. So beautiful. So fragile. Although she'd beat him up if he told her so.

His voice cracked when he spoke. "You're not stupid, dumb, dull, thick or even a moron. You're one of the smartest people I know. You're talented and skilled." He kissed the end of her nose and watched as unshed tears pooled in her eyes, making them sparkle. "There's a written test for becoming a caving leader, isn't there? That's why you haven't taken the exam."

She bit her bottom lip as she nodded.

"Oh, baby." Harry wrapped her in his arms and felt his heart ease as she wound hers around his waist.

"You won't tell anyone, will you, Harry?" she whispered against his neck. Her fear was like a knife to his gut.

Harry leaned up on his elbow to look down into her gorgeous face. She took his breath away. He gently caressed her cheek.

"There's nothing to tell," he said softly. "You aren't stupid. You've had a lot to deal with and I'm sorry I wasn't there to help you get through it."

One lone tear escaped and trailed down her cheek.

"Magenta." Harry pressed his nose to hers. "You're perfect the way you are. Nothing could make me think less of you. Nothing." He leaned back to look in her eyes. "You've got to know I love you, baby." Her breath hitched. He saw a flicker of hope before she masked it. "I do. I love you exactly as you are."

She started to shake her head. Denying his words.

"Sh." He pressed a gentle kiss to her lips. "Don't think about it. You don't have to say anything. Nothing you can say, or do, will change how I feel anyway. I came back for you, Magenta. I might be years too late, but I came back. And I do love you. Believe that. I do love you."

He lay on his back and pulled Magenta into his arms, where he held her close. For a long time they lay like that, listening to the silence, watching the shadows, until he felt Magenta fall asleep. Harry kissed the top of her head.

He'd help Magenta see that she was nothing like she'd described.

She was perfect.

And she was his.

CHAPTER 18

Magenta woke to find herself alone in bed and her clothing gone. She was dressed only in her underwear and had no recollection of taking her clothes off. Harry. She'd been so worn out after their chat that she'd slept like the dead. She groaned at the ceiling, wondering where he was now and feeling grateful that he'd left her with underwear.

The room tilted as she turned towards the clock by her bed. She had a hangover. An emotion hangover, which was the worst kind, because you still remembered every traumatic thing you did or said to get it. She glanced at the time, relieved to find that she had an hour before she was due at work.

The door was kicked open and a grinning Harry entered carrying a tray loaded with food. "I made breakfast."

His smile had a daze-inducing effect on her sanity. He was dressed in yesterday's jeans, but his feet and chest were bare. Magenta snatched the sheet and pulled it up to under her chin, making Harry laugh.

At the sight of him, memories of his whispered words

from the night before flooded her mind. He'd said he loved her. It didn't feel real. She wasn't convinced she hadn't dreamed the whole thing.

"What's with all the vegan stuff in the fridge?" He placed the tray on the bed beside her.

His words brought her back to the present.

"Megan's latest health kick." Magenta eyed the food. There was toast, a variety of spreads, eggs, bacon, sausages, mushrooms and potatoes. "How many people are you feeding?"

"Just us." He winked at her before handing her a plate loaded with food.

Magenta reached for the coffee and was grateful to find that it was mud thick. Exactly the way she liked it. She eyed Harry thoughtfully, feeling slightly nervous that they were hanging out half naked in her bedroom. Not that her body had a problem with this. No, her body wanted to rub against Harry's chest, to feel the muscles and sprinkling of hair against her skin. Her body wanted Harry's huge, skilled hands dancing over her. Her body wanted to be licked, and kissed, and touched. It took a great deal of effort to get her body to shut up.

She opened her mouth to thank Harry for the food and tell him to clear out. Unfortunately, that wasn't what came out. "How often do you work out?" she said instead.

She felt the blush heat her cheeks. He had way more than the two-pack he'd claimed in the mine. There were at least six well-defined muscles decorating his stomach. His biceps were firm enough to bite, but it was his wide shoulders that made her shudder. She was a sucker for a broad-shouldered man.

"Every day," he said through a mouthful of food. "Otherwise I'd spend 24/7 sitting at my computer and have a backside like Jabba the Hutt. Plus you don't want to be unfit and fight. MMA is gruelling. You need to be on top of your game physically as well as mentally—even when you're an amateur."

She thought about that as she nibbled on some toast. "Let me get this right. You compete at mixed martial arts, you run a company, you are the UK expert in security-based programming and you go rock climbing when you have free time." For some reason, all of that irritated her. "I hate to tell you, Harry, but your life screams *overachiever*. Are you good at everything you do?"

His eyes grew dark. "How about you find out the answer to that for yourself?"

Magenta swallowed hard as her body started screaming at her again. Her body had needs, it told her. Harry could satisfy those needs. Harry was good at everything. Her body was convinced he'd be *very* good at satisfying her. Magenta frowned at herself. She didn't have time to lust after Harry. There were things to be said.

"Harry, about what you said last night?" She couldn't seem to make any more words come out of her mouth.

His eyes twinkled. "I wondered how long it would take you to freak out about that."

She scowled at him. "I wanted you to know that I know you didn't mean it. That you were just comforting me after... after everything I told you. I wanted you to know that I'm okay with you not meaning it. People say things in the heat of the moment. I understand that."

His eyes went wide. "You think I told you I love you to make you feel better?"

She nodded. She couldn't think of another reason he might say it. He wiped a hand over his face.

"Those freaks from your past really did a number on you, didn't they?"

She wasn't sure what she was supposed to say to that, so she didn't say anything. Instead she bit her bottom lip and waited. Part of her wanted him to deny that he'd told her he loved her in the heat of the moment. Another part of her wanted him to agree. Her head was a mess.

"Baby." He reached for her hand and wound his fingers with hers. "I meant what I said. I came back for you. Not for the business. Rachel is right about that—it would probably be better if we kept our base in London. I don't care about that. I care about you. I love you. I wasn't lying. It's always been you for me."

Well, hell. She knew she was gaping at him, but words weren't forming in her head or her mouth. He loved her? He meant it? Was this real? Had she somehow fallen into one of the dreams she'd had as a kid?

Harry chuckled as he shook his head.

"Don't worry, you'll get used to it." His grin made her lick her lips. "Especially seeing as you're in love with me too."

Her back snapped straight. "I am not." Was she? Maybe. Probably. Who knows? Shouldn't she be the one figuring it out? Instead she had him telling her what she felt. She glared at him.

He flashed that sexy grin of his that needed to be outlawed. "You might as well admit it, baby. You love me."

Magenta narrowed her eyes at him. Irritating, frustrating, annoying man. "Don't tell me what I feel. And don't call me baby. Scottish men don't call their women baby. They use darling or pet, or who knows what the hell else. But *baby* is an American thing."

He grinned. "So you admit you're my woman?"

"No, I don't admit that. Listen to yourself. What century are you living in?" She lowered her voice to mimic his. "Me man. You woman. Me own you. You mine."

He laughed, which made her frown. Bloody caveman.

"I'm just saying," Magenta said, "that in general, Scottish men don't use *baby* as a term of endearment." And yes, she was more than aware that she was using this discussion to ignore the whole "I love you" thing. Her brain was not ready to deal with that yet. It might never be.

"Baby, I'm a child of a global culture. I watch more American TV than any other type. I was brainwashed into the American way before I could walk properly. I'm not ashamed to admit that I thought Captain Picard was my real father and the only reason he let my parents raise me was that he didn't want me on the *Enterprise*." He grinned. "Space can be dangerous for a kid. Look at all the stuff that happened to Wesley Crusher."

Magenta leaned forward and smacked him on the back of the head. Not hard. Just enough to snap him out of the weird little detour his brain was taking.

"As I was saying." He made a production of rubbing his head. "Welcome to the new world, where we all use American slang. You need to trust me on this—no matter where the term comes from, you are definitely my baby."

Magenta stared at him for a minute before blinking. She didn't know what to do with him. He wasn't fighting by any rules she knew. There was only one option. When in doubt—run.

"I've had enough of this. Time to get ready for work." She moved to throw back the covers but remembered she was only wearing her underwear. "Throw me a T-shirt, will you?"

He cocked an eyebrow at her. "Why? I've seen it all before." His grin was lascivious. "I like the pink lingerie. It was a nice surprise to find a Disney princess under Xena the Warrior Princess."

"You are such a geek."

"And proud of it." He waggled his eyebrows while he reached for his T-shirt. Of course he was going to be all macho and dress her in his clothes, even though she was in a room full of her own.

Magenta shrugged into it. Some arguments weren't worth the effort. She threw back the covers and strode past Harry. His arm shot out to stop her. She glared at him.

"You're forgetting something."

"What?" She let out a long-suffering sigh.

"Our morning kiss." His eyes twinkled with mischief.

"Harry, we're not in a relationship."

"Whatever you want to believe. Kiss me good morning anyway." He pulled her close until she was standing between his knees. His arms wrapped tightly around her waist. "I'm not letting go until I get my morning kiss."

"Fine, you stubborn pervert." Magenta put a hand on each of his shoulders, leaned forward and pecked him on the cheek. "Good morning, Harry," she said with fake cheer.

His eyes narrowed and she almost laughed. She'd forgotten about this. Forgotten how much fun it was to play with him.

"I want a real kiss," he growled.

"That's as good as it's getting. Take it or leave it."

"Coward."

"Bully."

"Scaredy-cat."

"Man-whore."

He cocked an eyebrow. "Man-whore?"

She shrugged. "I heard all about your many relationships over the years." Each one had chipped away at her soul. "It kind of makes a mockery of your claim that I've always been the one for you. Your string of girlfriends says otherwise. Who knows where those lips of yours have been."

"I thought you didn't want me, then someone told me otherwise. Those women were nothing but placeholders." He gave her a slow grin. "You're jealous."

"Am not."

"Oh, you are so."

"I'm going to thump you in a minute."

"Now, now, Magenta, you need to work at controlling that temper of yours. What would happen to your reputation if it got out that Invertary's badass was too scared to kiss her man because she was in a snit about the other women he'd dated? That doesn't sound like a badass to me. That sounds like a big old cowardly chicken." He started making chicken noises.

Magenta dug her nails into his bare shoulders. It didn't stop the clucking. Or the grinning.

"You're not my man. Stop making a fool of yourself," she ordered. He didn't.

His tight hold meant she couldn't get away from him. His mocking was driving her nuts. "I swear, Harry, stop that stupid noise or I'll stop it for you."

He actually chuckled while he clucked like a chicken. So Magenta shut him up the only way she could think of—she slammed her mouth down on his.

Harry hummed with delight, and then, being the great big control freak that he was, he took over the kiss. Magenta was past caring. As soon as her lips touched Harry's, her annoyance evaporated. She didn't even care enough to be irritated that she was hopelessly easy when it came to the man. Nope, all she cared about was getting closer to him.

She felt like she was falling down a vertical shaft, into the darkness and the unknown—without a lifeline.

And the feeling was addictive.

In that moment, with the taste of Harry on her tongue and his warm, solid muscle under her fingertips, she wasn't sure if she would ever let him go. Common sense told her that her sanity would return when his lips left hers. But while they were touching, while he was kissing her, she chose to believe that he was right. That they were soul mates. That Harry could get past the fact he was so much more intelligent than she was. That they could have a future together. Not just any future, but the one she'd dreamed of as a kid.

The one where she got to keep Harry. Forever.

Harry's brain, which usually had a million thoughts working through it at any given time, narrowed its focus to only one thought—Magenta. Only she had the power to stop him thinking about anything but her. Her lips tasted like honey and were as soft as petals, but the way she kissed wasn't flower delicate. It was a devouring. He loved every second of it.

Magenta's fingers worked their way into his overgrown hair and tugged. The tingle in his scalp made him grateful that he rarely remembered to get a haircut. If this was what it felt like to have Magenta hold on to him, then he was keeping his hair long from now on. She gasped into his mouth as his hands slid under her T-shirt to caress her back. Her warm, smooth skin was like heaven. He could spend days caressing each and every inch of her.

With a flick of his wrist, he unsnapped her bra. She made a little growling noise and deepened the kiss. Damn, her taste was addictive. Gasping for air, Harry broke the kiss. As fast as he could, he whisked the T-shirt and bra over her head, before she had time to protest. One look into her desire-filled eyes and he knew protesting was the last thing on her mind.

"Admit you love me," Harry ordered.

Her hands massaged his shoulders, nails digging in and sending spikes of need throughout his body. "Get over yourself, Harry. You're not that irresistible." Magenta's voice was husky and slightly dazed. He smiled against the curve of her neck at the sound.

Breathing deeply of the fragrance that was pure Magenta, he nipped the spot where her shoulder curved into neck and was rewarded by a moan. Her fingers tightened on his shoulders.

"Say you love me," he said against her skin before he sucked, hoping to leave a mark. "We both know you do. You might as well admit it."

Her breasts pressed against his chest. She wriggled to make her nipples rub against his hair and murmured in delight. Harry licked a path along her shoulder as he kept his arms tight around her.

"Come on, Magenta, tell me you love me," he said. "You know you want to."

He angled her back and glanced at her face. The emotion he saw there stopped his heart. He couldn't breathe. Couldn't think. He was transfixed. The depth of Magenta's feelings for him were written in her eyes. They stared at each other for long moments. But still Magenta didn't speak. With a small smile, Harry broke eye contact, leaned forward and sucked her nipple. Her fingers flew back to his hair as she held on tight. Harry swirled the peak with his tongue. Her moan almost made him lose control.

"Give in, say the words."

He kissed and sucked and nibbled on her gorgeous flesh, listening with delight as she whimpered and gasped. He felt her shiver under his touch, and sway as her knees weakened. It made him want to roar with delight.

"Not. Going. To. Happen." Her words were spat out between gasping breaths. "You. Can't. Make. Me. Say. It."

He let her nipple go with a satisfying pop as he leaned back to look at her flushed face.

"Is that a challenge?" He could tell by the wide-eyed look that his grin was as wicked as he felt.

Slowly, she smiled back at him with an answering sparkle of mischief in her eyes.

"Bring your A-game, Harry boy—there's no way you'll make me say anything I don't want to."

With a laugh, he picked her up and threw her back on to the bed. She bounced once with a squeal before he pressed his weight alongside her.

"A-game it is, then," he told her before capturing her lips with his.

MAGENTA WAS SMILING when Harry kissed her. Nothing would stop him now. His cavemanly honour was at stake. If she wasn't giddy with the taste of his decadent lips, she would have giggled.

His big hand smoothed down her side, over the outer curve of her breast, her hip, until it slid under her thigh. He pulled her leg up to him, making space for his hips in the cradle of her thighs. The soft blue jeans he still wore felt almost abrasive against her skin. She wanted them gone. She wanted to feel all of him.

Her fingers danced over the shoulders she loved, and trailed over back muscles that trembled with strength. She wanted to memorise every dip and curve.

"Say it," he growled against her throat.

"Nuh-uh." She shook her head. Her eyes closed. A grin on her face.

He bit the tendon on her neck, hard, and Magenta saw stars. Her insides melted.

"Again," she ordered.

"Say you love me and I'll do it again."

Mean. That was just mean. Fine. Two could play at that game. She pressed upwards, tucking her face into his neck. She licked a trail from his shoulder to his ear before grasping his earlobe in her teeth. His breathing was strained. His muscles taut.

"Are you sure you aren't the one who's going to give in under pressure?" she whispered against his ear.

He shuddered, growled like an animal. That made her laugh. A laugh that stopped abruptly when his hand curved around her breast and his mouth descended on her nipple. She was so sensitive to his touch that it was almost painful. He sucked hard. Her body bowed beneath him. The moan she made torn from her throat. Her fingers clinging to his shoulders.

"Say it. Say you love me," he rasped against her.

"I. Love…" He sucked in a breath as he stilled over her. "Your shoulders."

He growled as she laughed and gasped and moaned in quick succession. She was delirious with wanting him. More than that, she was having fun with him, and that delighted everything within her.

"Evil woman." He nipped her breast. "Obviously I need to up the stakes."

He crawled down her body until he was kneeling between her legs. She should have felt self-conscious as he studied her, but the desire in his eyes made her feel needy.

"Now." He traced his finger along the edge of her underwear. "What would make you surrender fastest?" His smile was so sexy it should have been banned.

"Nothing. There's nothing you can do that will get me to say the words you want." She fought a giggle.

"Fighting words." His thumbs hooked under her underwear at her hips.

Slowly, oh so slowly, he peeled them down, moving back off the bed so he could get them off her. He stood at the end of the bed while she lay naked before him. Spread out like dessert at a buffet.

"Take off your jeans," she ordered.

He cocked an eyebrow. "I don't think you're in any position to make demands. Tell me you love me and I'll take them off."

She laughed so hard her whole body shook. "Isn't that cutting your nose off to spite your face? Don't you want your jeans off?"

His cheeks flushed red. "Damn it, Magenta, you make my IQ drop to double digits. It's impossible to think straight around you."

She took that as a compliment. Grumbling, he removed his jeans and underpants. She sucked in a breath as he stood before her. Six foot two of solid, delicious man.

"You like?"

"Oh yeah." She couldn't take her eyes off him.

"You want?"

"Oh yeah."

With a cocky grin, he crawled up her body until his face loomed over hers. He held himself above her on hands and knees. "Well, all you have to do is say the words, and all this is yours."

Magenta laughed until her stomach ached. Harry stayed perched above her, waiting patiently.

"Stupid man," she said at last. "It's all mine anyway."

She ran her hands over his chest and stomach. He stiffened, waiting to see what she would do. Heady from the power she had over him, Magenta wrapped a hand around his shaft.

"Oh, hell," he groaned. His head fell forward until his forehead rested on hers. "This is not going the way I planned."

Magenta arched up as her hands stroked his hot flesh and her tongue licked along his bottom lip. "Your A-game sucks, Harry. You're never going to get me to say what you want like this. You're putty in my hands. Literally." She gave him a squeeze to make her point.

Magenta loved the bewildered, yet desperate, look on his face. Poor Harry. He wasn't going to win, and he didn't know what to do about it. She was congratulating herself on a game well played when he suddenly moved backwards out of her grasp. Magenta let out a whine of complaint.

With a grin, he crawled back down her body and off the bed. Magenta frowned at him.

"Are you giving up? Do I win?"

"You're about to."

Before she could process his words, he fell to his knees at the side of the bed. Strong hands curved around her ankles as he yanked her down until her backside rested on the edge of the bed.

He looked up at her, his eyes skimming over her body. He licked his lips. "If you want to come, you need to say the magic words."

He palmed her thighs wide.

"Bastard!" Magenta said. Her insult was way too breathless to be of any use.

"That's not the magic word," he admonished before his head descended.

At the first touch of his tongue, Magenta almost flew off

the bed. Only his strength kept her in place. Her mind spun as her body writhed under him. She couldn't think. She definitely couldn't talk. All she could do was feel. And oh my goodness, what a feeling. Her hands clawed at the bedding as she panted her desire. Nearly there. Damn. Her muscles began to spasm, her head felt light, her breath caught in her throat. And then—nothing.

He stopped. She strained to open her eyes. He was sitting back on his heels, grinning at her.

"You want the prize, you need to tell me you love me."

"Go to hell." This wasn't fun anymore. She'd been so close. It was mean to deny her. She almost pouted at the thought.

The evil genius laughed. "Ready for round two?"

Magenta wanted to smack him, but she honestly didn't have the energy. Her body was wired, desperate for release. She decided to take matters into her own hands. Literally. As her hand moved down her stomach, Harry grabbed it.

"Uh-uh, that's cheating." He gathered both her wrists in one of his hands and held them tight on her stomach. "If you want that big O, you need to say the magic words."

"You're going to pay for this," she said. It was pathetically weak.

"I hope so," he said before his mouth moved back to teasing her.

He sucked, he licked, he nipped. Magenta fought to move her hips. Fought for the release that was just there, sitting out of reach.

He sat back again. At least he was breathing hard. It was good to know she wasn't the only one affected.

"Magenta," he growled.

"Fine. Do it. I'll say the words."

"Say them first."

"I love…" She took a deep breath, ready to say it, but her

sick sense of humour got the better of her. "I love Harry Potter," she shouted.

Her giggle was cut short when his tongue touched her again. She honestly couldn't take any more.

"Fine. Fine. I love you, Hairy Boil, I love you."

The words released a pressure valve of emotion within her. Every feeling she'd had for him over the years burst forth. Everything she'd buried or denied. Oh how she loved this man.

His forehead rested on her lower stomach, and she felt him relax. "You bet your life you love me." He sounded smug.

Magenta lifted her head. She blinked back tears of hope that threatened, and aimed for sounding lighthearted. "Are you going to finish this now?"

"Oh yeah." Harry gave her a satisfied grin.

His skilled lips and tongue devoured her, and ten seconds later she was flying. The world disappeared. Perfect. It was perfect. When she came back to earth, she was lying sprawled on the bed with Harry over her. The heat from his skin soothed her. He brushed her hair away from her face, placing a kiss on her nose.

"I love you too, Magenta," he said against her lips.

Her heart stuttered at the words. Hope bloomed within her. She wanted him. She wanted to believe they could get past their differences. She wanted it so much it hurt.

Slowly, she felt him inch inside her. Harry. Her Harry. The only man she'd ever loved. He'd been everything to her. Her whole world. She wanted that again. Desperately. His soft kisses snatched her gasps and moans as he joined with her.

"I love you," he told her again. "Only you. Forever."

The words were said solemnly. A promise she was desperate to believe. As he held himself on straining arms above her, Magenta cupped his face in her hands.

"I do love you, you bully," she said.

His grin was pure sunshine. "One of these days you'll tell me without insulting me at the same time."

That made her laugh. A laugh that turned into a desperate gasp as he moved within her. She wrapped her arms around him and let herself drift away, floating on waves of sensation.

Perfect.

CHAPTER 20

Harry was buzzing from making love to Magenta. If he'd had his way, he'd have never let her out of bed. He could still feel her on his skin. Feel her wrapped around him. It was like nothing he'd ever experienced before. He had no words for it. Except *perfection.*

He'd smiled when she'd come down from the high of making love. After her shower, she was grumpy and annoyed. Although she didn't say it, he was pretty sure she was mad that she'd admitted her feelings. He could live with that. He was under no illusions as to how stubborn his woman could be. His woman. He grinned at the thought. Man, he loved that crazy girl so much it hurt.

When Magenta had stomped off to work, complaining that she was late and protesting that words said under duress didn't count, Harry headed to his meeting with Rachel. They were looking at the office space again. He planned to sign the lease then go over to the local secondary school to talk to Magenta's old English teacher.

He was certain Magenta was dyslexic. Harry had a friend in London who was dyslexic, a very successful and intelligent friend. Harry knew the signs. He also knew that it wasn't related to IQ. The fact Magenta had come to believe she was stupid because of it made him want to punch something. Or someone. Lots of someones.

"What are you frowning at?" Rachel said.

They were checking out the new office space one last time before Harry signed the lease.

"Something Magenta said that I didn't like." More accurately, something the people around her had told her time and again. It made him cold with rage to think about it.

Rachel folded her arms over a severe royal-blue shift dress and tapped the toe of her red Louboutin shoe on the linoleum-covered floor. He knew they were Louboutin shoes because Rachel had given him a lecture on the designer's trademark being red leather soles. To say that Harry couldn't have cared less would have been putting it mildly.

"Aren't you finished chasing that girl?" She waved a dismissive hand. "Let's forget this lease thing and move back to London, where we have a perfectly decent office set up. One that's close to Sloane Square instead of being close to Invertary's only pub." She sniffed in disgust.

"Stop being such a snob, Rachel. The landscape here is beautiful. The air is fresh. People fight to live in places like this."

"Some of us would rather be surrounded by culture."

He rolled his eyes, making sure she saw it. "There's culture here. Scottish culture. You don't get better than that."

"Save me the Braveheart speeches. We've had enough of that for one trip."

Harry walked over to the window that looked out over the loch and smiled. This was the spot he'd set up his machines. That way, when he looked up from his latest code he could stare out at the blue water and lush green hills.

"Set it up. We'll sign today," he told her.

"I really have to object. Again. You only want to do this because you have a hard-on for the Goth. Is that a reason to move your company? She doesn't even want you. Why can't you take the hint and let us go home?"

"She does want me. She's been protecting me. She thinks she isn't smart enough to date me. She's had issues with reading and writing, and from what she says I think she's dyslexic. That's something I can help her with. Once that problem is gone, she won't worry about us being too different to make a relationship work."

"She isn't smart enough for you. Most people aren't. For the love of all things Gucci, you have an IQ that reads like a phone number. People are queuing up to get at your latest code. You see holes in programming security most experts would never see. And she"—Rachel huffed in disgust —"works in a shop and likes to play in an abandoned mine. From what you say, I doubt she even knows how to turn a computer on. Have you thought about her in all of this? Mmm? If your intelligence intimidates her, how upset would she be around your friends? Your colleagues? You aren't doing her any favours throwing her into a world she barely understands. It will only make her feel more inadequate."

Harry thought about that for a minute as his stomach churned. Would it hurt her? Her self-esteem had taken a kicking these past few years. Maybe pushing her to deal with his overly educated circle of friends was a bad idea. He shook his head. Magenta wasn't that easily intimidated. He wasn't going to think like this.

"It will be fine," Harry said. "Get the paperwork for the lease and I'll sign it."

"Are you sure?" Rachel cocked an eyebrow at him. "Self-esteem is a delicate thing. If your girl is worried she isn't clever enough for you, then she may never get over that."

"I'm sure." Harry strode towards the door. "I'm going to help her. It will all be fine, you'll see."

With that, he left Rachel to deal with the lease and headed to the local high school to have a word with his old English teacher, Mrs. Adams. Maybe together they could find a way to fix the damage in Magenta's past.

MAGENTA WAS IN A BAD MOOD. She was also late for work, which didn't help her disposition any. She was annoyed that she'd caved and told Harry she loved him—even if it was true. It didn't solve anything. She was still the village idiot and he was still the genius boy wonder. No matter how much she'd convinced herself that they had a future, she knew they didn't. It was a delusion brought on by lust. Lust and his really talented tongue.

To complement her mood, she'd worn her "leave me alone" outfit to work. Black mini-skirt, black bat-wing top with the words "Back Off Bitch" written in red across her chest, a studded dog collar, studded belt, red tartan tights and black Doc Marten boots. She'd painted her eyes with even more eyeliner than usual and coated her nails with blood-red polish.

"Excellent, you made the effort to turn up. Well done," Kirsty said when she arrived.

Magenta ignored the sarcasm. "I'm sorry."

"Want to give me a reason for you being late?"

What was this? School? No, she didn't want to give a reason. Especially when that reason involved her being in bed with Harry. The town already knew too much about her sex life without her adding to it.

Kirsty sighed. "I see you're all decked out to be delightful to my customers."

Magenta growled. "I was going to strap a knife to my thigh. I didn't."

Kirsty's eyes went wide. "And that's supposed to make me feel grateful?"

Magenta stomped over to the new posters that were to go up in the store window. Each one showed a perfectly stunning Victoria's Secret model. She hated them all.

"Who put the bug up your bum?" Kirsty said. "Come on. What's the problem?"

Magenta almost cracked a smile. Kirsty never said things like that. She glared at her friend. "Harry." Magenta figured one word was enough.

Kirsty let out a dramatic sigh. She was going for a wood nymph look in a leaf-green chiffon top with long, billowing sleeves, over beige suede trousers. With her red hair and green eyes, she was beyond stunning. Exactly like the models on the posters. Not fair. Not fair at all. Damn, everything was getting to her. Now Magenta thought she didn't look good enough for Harry. She growled at herself, irritated that her thoughts were so girly.

"Why won't you date the guy?" Kirsty said. "You might be surprised and actually enjoy it."

She was glad Kirsty didn't know exactly how much she enjoyed Harry.

"Harry doesn't want to date. He wants to get straight to the marriage and baby part. He's come back for his soul mate. He thinks it's me. He's never done things by halves. So dating him won't work."

"Marriage? Babies? Did he say that?" Kirsty's voice was an insulting squeak.

"More like implied it, with the 'you're mine forever,' 'we were made for each other' comments he keeps making."

"You and Harry, having babies? Children? Heaven help us. Miniature computer geniuses who dress only in black and hate almost everyone who crosses their paths. The world wouldn't be safe. On second thoughts, don't date Harry. Run from him. Run fast."

"Funny," Magenta told her friend and boss. "Very funny." Magenta figured that with her being so stupid and Harry being so smart, their kids might end up with an IQ somewhere in the middle. They might actually be normal. She almost screamed. Why the hell was she thinking about kids? She was twenty-one. Too young to get married. Too young to have children. And definitely too young to deal with someone who thought he was her soul mate.

"He said he loves me," she found herself telling Kirsty. Her mouth would not stay shut. It was like a compulsion, this sudden need to bare her soul.

She heard a thud, and turned to find Kirsty had dropped the box of hangers she'd been holding.

"I told him I love him too. It came out under duress." She was still annoyed about that.

"So, you don't love him?"

She shook her head then sighed. Why not go the whole hog and wail too? "No, I do love him. I've always loved him. I just don't see how we can have a future. We're too different. I couldn't even finish high school, whereas Harry has a whole alphabet after his name."

Kirsty came up beside her and squeezed her shoulder. "There's all kinds of intelligence, Magenta. Just because you didn't do well in academia, doesn't mean you're ignorant. You can do things Harry can't do."

"Like?"

"Like get within three miles of a rat." Kirsty grinned.

Magenta smiled back at her friend as the worry within her lessened some. "Heard about that, huh?"

"Wish I'd seen it." Kirsty looked almost wistful.

"I think Claire saved the file. She can email it to you. It might be up on YouTube by now anyway."

Kirsty gave her shoulders another squeeze. "Don't worry about things so much. They have a way of working out. And don't think you are any less than Harry because he has degrees and you don't. That's a crazy way to think."

Magenta shrugged out from under her friend's arm. "You're right. I'm turning into a sissy."

Kirsty shook her head. "Not what I said." She moved to pick up the box she'd dropped, her eyes straying to the shop door. "Customer," Kirsty told her. "Try not to scare her away."

"I can't promise anything." Magenta turned to the front of the shop and her heart sank. Excellent. Executive Barbie. Magenta didn't bother plastering a fake smile on her face. Rachel wasn't worth the effort.

Harry's friend and business manager sailed through the door like a despot ruler gracing the plebs with her presence.

"Magenta." It was amazing how much distaste she could squeeze into one word. "I'd like to have a word with you about Harry."

"Again?" Magenta rolled her eyes dramatically. The twins would have been proud. "Haven't we already done this? I can't even begin to express how *not* interested I am in doing it again."

"Be that as it may," Rachel said, and Magenta took a minute to wonder how there were actually people out there that said that kind of thing. "But Harry is about to sign a lease on new office space, and I can't allow that to happen. Moving to Invertary is a mistake. We both know that." Her lip actually curled up when she said "Invertary."

"I don't know if it's a mistake or not, Rachel. I'm not involved with your business."

"Exactly." She tapped her chin, flashing her perfect French manicure. "Harry did mention that the workings of the business would be over your head. He said that you hadn't even finished high school." Her smile was cold. "Please forgive me if what I'm about to explain is difficult for you to comprehend. I'm more used to dealing with people who are educated."

Magenta was vaguely aware of Kirsty sucking in a shocked breath. She ignored it as she clenched her fists into tight, tension-filled balls by her side.

Magenta ground her teeth. "Do you have a point?"

Rachel's eyes turned cold and her voice dropped. Her haughty tone was gone.

"My point is that you need to back off from Harry. He's got a life in London, a business to run, contracts to fulfil. People depending on him. Instead of spending his time dealing with all of that, he's chasing his high school crush. A crush who has made it painfully obvious she isn't suited to him." She folded her arms and drummed her fingers on her biceps. "Tell him to go to London. Tell him there's no chance with you. Make it clear. And for the love of all things Prada, do it before he ties us to a lease on an office that none of us want."

Magenta worked to take calming breaths. Whatever was happening, or not happening, between her and Harry was their business. No one else's. His designer sidekick didn't have the right to stick her nose in.

"And if I don't do this?" Magenta's tone was ice.

Rachel smirked. An honest-to-goodness, superior-as-all-out smirk. Magenta's blood shot past boiling and straight to red steam. She was sure it spewed from her ears.

"I don't know what game you're playing with Harry, but do you honestly think you'll fit into his world? That his friends will accept you? You won't even understand the conversations we have. You can't even read and write."

Kirsty made a strangled noise. Magenta froze. Rachel smiled. Cold. Calculating.

"That's right. He told me. The love of his life is so thick she can't even read and write. A perfect match for one of the brightest brains of this generation, don't you think?"

Every insecurity Magenta struggled with surged to the forefront of her mind. Her dirty secret was out. Now Kirsty knew that she'd hired an idiot. The thought burned. It actually physically burned. A searing pain in her stomach. How could Harry have done this to her? No. He couldn't have. This wasn't the kind of thing Harry would do. He'd never gossip about her to Rachel. Something else was going on here.

Rachel leaned in towards her. "Face facts, little girl—you are far too stupid for Harry. You will drag him down and everyone will get hurt. He's too busy and important to waste time explaining every tiny little thing to you in small words so you can understand. Let him go to London and you can stay here, selling underwear and pretending you aren't as dumb as you look."

"Oh hell," Kirsty wailed.

Magenta barely noticed her cry. All she saw was that smirk on Rachel's face, and the next thing she knew, her fist was flying straight for it.

CHAPTER 21

Harry was in the middle of an enlightening conversation with his high school English teacher when his phone rang. He apologised profusely as he reached for it, thinking it would be work. He was puzzled to see Kirsty's name on the screen.

"Hey, Kirsty," he said as he smiled at Mrs. Adams.

"Get your backside to my shop right now. You need to stop Magenta from killing Rachel. Oh crap, got to go."

The line went dead. Harry stared at the phone for a second. What the…?

"I'm sorry, I need to go. Kirsty said Magenta is in a fight at the lingerie shop." He could hardly believe the words came out of his mouth.

Mrs. Adams didn't look surprised. "Some things never change. That girl has always had a short fuse, especially if someone called her an idiot."

Harry's stomach tried to climb out of his oesophagus as the blood drained from his face. Rachel wouldn't. Would she? He hung his head. He should never have told Rachel about Magenta's dyslexia.

"I need to run. Now."

He was out of the door at a sprint as Mrs. Adams called out her goodbyes behind him.

The high school, like everything else in Invertary, wasn't far from the main street. It took Harry less than five minutes to get to Kirsty's shop. What he saw made him screech to a halt.

On the floor, in the middle of a completely trashed lingerie shop, were two wrestling women. Magenta's T-shirt was ripped, flashing a fuchsia-coloured bra. Her hair was wild and there was a crazy glint in her eye. Rachel's designer dress was up around her hips, allowing everyone to see that she was wearing underwear from Kirsty's new pink tartan line. There was a scrape on her thigh and it looked like her manicured fingernails were broken. She was also missing one of those red-soled shoes she loved so much. Magenta was on Rachel's back, trying to strangle Rachel with a green satin bra. Rachel, in turn, had a death grip on a leg that had broken off a mannequin. She was using it to pummel Magenta. The noise was phenomenal. He'd heard quieter catfights.

Harry's jaw fell open as he spotted his cousin Matt, in full police gear, and Kirsty's fiancé Lake standing off to the side. Both men were grinning as they watched the fight.

"Why the hell aren't you stopping this?" Harry shouted at them.

"We tried," Matt said. "Magenta kicked me with those bloody boots she has on. I think they have steel toe caps."

"Rachel bit me." Lake held up his hand, which had a Band-Aid on it.

"We decided to enjoy the show until they ran out of steam," Matt said.

"Not every day you see women wrestling in a lingerie shop." Lake let loose with a full-blown grin. "I told Kirsty to film it. Rachel's wearing one of Kirsty's designs. She could use this for publicity."

Matt nodded. "I'd watch it again. Especially since they started using lingerie as weapons."

"We need to break this up," Harry told the idiots. "Kirsty's shop is getting trashed."

"Yep," Lake said. "You're paying to have it fixed." He pointed at the women. "This is your mess."

Before Harry could reply, Kirsty came barrelling through from the back of the shop, carrying a bucket.

"Out of my way, you perverts," she shouted.

The men stepped aside. Lake eyed the bucket.

"You're a genius," he told his fiancée. He turned to Matt. "What would make this better?"

They grinned like idiots. "Water," they said at the same time.

Harry was about to step in and haul Magenta off Rachel—well, try to, anyway—but Kirsty was too fast. She emptied the bucket of cold water over the two women. There was coughing and spluttering. The women broke apart as they wiped water from their eyes. Rachel tried to stand, but slid on the wet floor. It took her two more attempts before she was on her feet, and then she realised her dress was around her waist. With a growl, she yanked it back down. Magenta sat on the floor, wiping her face on the edge of her T-shirt.

"Was that really necessary?" Magenta snapped at Kirsty.

Kirsty stood with her hands on her hips, her green eyes blazing. "Was it necessary to trash my shop because you have anger management issues?"

Harry looked around at the sodden underwear that littered the floor. Kirsty had a point.

"She started it," Magenta complained.

"What are you? Five?" Kirsty looked like she was going to restart the fight herself. "Get this place fixed. I want it perfect." She turned to Harry, who held up his hands in surrender. "You too. This is your mess. I'm surrounded by juvenile idiots who hit first and think later." She spun on Lake and Matt. "You two are no better. You could have stopped this before the damage got this bad." She pointed at Lake. "Consider your sex life on hold for the foreseeable future."

"Kirsty, love…" Lake's face paled with worry.

"Don't 'Kirsty, love' me, Lake Benson. You wanted to watch the show. Well, now you can pay for it too."

Kirsty held her head high as she stomped to the back of the shop and the stairs to her apartment. Everyone watched her leave, then, as one, the three men folded their arms and turned to the two soaked women.

"Now I'm annoyed," Lake said as he watched her go.

"Assault, criminal damage, vandalism," Matt said. "Those are only the charges I can think of off the top of my head. I could add public nudity, seeing as you've both been flashing your wares for the past twenty minutes. If I could charge you with stupidity, I would." He shook his head. "Give me one reason why I shouldn't haul the two of you back to my jail?"

"Because we're sorry?" Rachel said hopefully.

Matt gaze was cold. "Are you?"

"I am." Rachel sounded firm. It would have held more authority if she'd had on both shoes and wasn't soaking wet.

"Magenta?" Matt cocked an eyebrow at her where she still sat in a puddle on the floor.

She looked defiant. "I'm not sorry. I'd kick her skinny backside again in a heartbeat. She's a cold-hearted, manipulative witch."

Matt pinched the bridge of his nose. "Lake, what do you want? Do you want to press charges, seeing as you co-own the shop?"

The Englishman studied the women. "It's tempting. These two have kicked me out of Kirsty's bed."

"Technically you did that all by yourself," Magenta pointed out. "If you weren't such a big pervert you'd still be in her bed."

Lake made a little growling sound, although his face showed no emotion. "I want this place cleaned. Pristine. I want the damage paid for." He turned to Harry. "Sort this. I have more important things to deal with." He turned on his heels and stalked from the shop, heading to the apartment he shared with Kirsty.

"You heard the man," Matt said. "Looks like you get off with a warning. This time." He glared at Magenta. "It's time you grew up. You're an adult. You and those twit sisters of mine need to start acting like grown-ups. No more kids' pranks. No more sorting your problems with your fists. No more hiding from people instead of dealing with things. I've had enough of this. Am I making myself clear?"

Magenta gave a reluctant nod.

Matt turned to Rachel. "Stop playing people. Or I will run you out of town. Got it?"

Rachel nodded as her cheeks flushed red.

"On that note"—Matt adjusted his police hat—"I'm out of here. Harry, you're in charge. Make sure there isn't any more trouble." He strode to the door, but turned as he opened it. "Ladies, thanks for the show. It made my day." With a cheeky grin, he disappeared.

Slowly, the two women turned their gazes to Harry.

"Right," Harry said, "who's going to explain first?"

Magenta stared at her shoes. It wasn't going to be her. No way. The last thing she needed was the embarrassment of telling Harry she'd lost it because Rachel called her dumb. She *was* dumb. Rachel wasn't wrong. Still, it hurt that Harry had run straight to his friend and told her all about how stupid Magenta was. So no. She wasn't going to talk. Probably never again.

She peeked at Rachel. From the look on her face, she wasn't going to talk either. Guess Harry was out of luck.

His jaw clenched as he frowned at them. His shoulders flexed, making Magenta's mouth inappropriately water. She rolled her eyes at herself. Apparently her body was programmed to react to Harry no matter the circumstances. Harry growled. That was kind of sexy too. Magenta wanted to smack herself on the forehead.

Harry glared at Rachel. "Did you run over here to tell Magenta I thought she was dyslexic?"

Everything within Magenta stilled. What? Her eyes

snapped to Harry. He was still glaring at Rachel, who was staring at the floor like a naughty school kid.

"Rachel?" he rumbled.

"No. I didn't mention that." Rachel was speaking to her feet.

Magenta's heart thudded. She was missing something. Something important.

"What's dyslexic?" she asked Harry.

His eyes shot to hers, and his expression softened. "It's a learning disorder. It means you have problems processing written words. Your brain deals with language differently than most people. It can make it harder to read and write. It isn't a reflection on intelligence. Einstein was dyslexic—so were Picasso and Agatha Christie. Tom Cruise and Richard Branson are too."

He crouched down in front of her. Thoughts were zooming through Magenta's mind so fast she could barely keep track of them. Harry's eyes darkened with intimacy as he reached out to tuck her hair behind her ear.

"After what you told me, I thought you might be dyslexic. So I went to talk to Mrs. Adams. She agreed. That was the assessment she wanted to have done when you were in high school. She wanted you to be officially designated as dyslexic. That way you would have had the help you needed in school. She said you were—are—exceptionally bright. All you needed was some support with reading and writing."

"They weren't going to send me away?" Her voice was barely a whisper.

"No." Harry cupped her cheek, the warmth of his palm soothing. "No one was going to send you away. That was your mother's imagination. She has a lot to answer for. Being assessed would have meant you'd get more time on tests, maybe someone to read things to you. You'd learn tricks to cope with writing. That sort of thing."

Magenta stared at Harry for a long time. His smile was gentle and reassuring. He didn't push her to process. A rush of emotions hit Magenta hard. The strongest one being hope. She blinked at Harry, almost scared to talk in case the emotions slipped out and overwhelmed her.

"You really didn't know about dyslexia?" he said.

"I dropped out of school when I was thirteen, Harry. All I've worried about since then was how to hide my problems. Maybe if I'd talked to a teacher, or my doctor, I might have heard of dyslexia, but the last thing I wanted to do was draw attention to myself." She looked up at him. "I'm not stupid am I?"

"No, baby, you're far from stupid."

"I'm not stupid." Magenta said, more to herself than anyone else. To her shame, a tear escaped and rolled down her cheek.

"Aw, baby," Harry muttered. He sat on the floor, right in the water, and pulled Magenta onto his lap. His arms engulfed her, offering comfort and protection. Two things Magenta normally shunned.

She knew she should have objected. She knew how weak it made her look to be held like a child, especially in front of Rachel, but she didn't care. She needed the contact, the support. In the seconds it'd taken Harry to tell her there was a reason for her difficulties, her whole world had changed. Everything she'd thought was real had been wiped away. She wasn't sure who she was anymore. She'd spent her life thinking she wasn't as clever as those around her; it would take some time to believe otherwise. As the weight of feeling inferior began to lift, hope that she might be normal blossomed in her mind. She rested her cheek on Harry's chest and let him comfort her as her brain raced.

"There are these glasses you can get," Harry said softly. "They have coloured lenses and they help to stop the words from dancing around the page. We'll get you some of those. There's also a society for people with dyslexia, they have loads of information on their website to help people cope. There are strategies you can use. We'll go through them together. Dyslexia is different for each person. Some people have more issues to deal with than others, but all of it can be handled with support. It shouldn't stop you doing anything you want to in life."

Her heart stilled. She looked up at Harry. Her stomach clenched as she dared hope. "I can take the caving tests?"

"Yeah, baby, you can take the tests. We'll tell them you're dyslexic and they'll accommodate you."

Magenta buried her face in Harry's shoulder. "I can become an instructor. Maybe start my own holiday caving business. I've always wanted to do that. I didn't dare think about it. I knew it would never happen. I knew I was too stupid."

"Sh. You aren't stupid. You're smart and talented and creative and ingenious. Nothing's going to stop you now. You can dream all you like."

He kissed the top of her head as his arms wrapped tightly around her.

Someone cleared their throat, and Magenta remembered that Rachel was still in the room. She couldn't look at the woman who had deliberately tried to hurt her.

"You two go," Rachel said. "I'll clean up."

Harry glared at his friend. "That won't make up for what you did. You betrayed my trust and attacked Magenta."

"She hit me first," Rachel snapped.

"You hurt her first. You came here to make her think she was stupid. That's cruel. I'm not sure what's going on in your head. I'm not sure who you are anymore. You and I are going to have a long talk later."

"Yeah." Rachel sounded defeated. "That's probably a good idea."

As Harry helped Magenta to her feet, she saw the look of shame on Rachel's face. It helped soften the animosity Magenta held.

"I think," Rachel said to Harry, but her eyes were on Magenta, "I should go back to London and head up the office there. You need to stay here."

"I think that's a good idea," Harry told her as he grabbed Magenta's hand and hauled her towards the door. "We're still going to talk, though. I'm not sure I trust you the way I used to, and that will affect business."

Rachel's cheeks turned red. As they reached the door, Magenta pulled out of Harry's grip. "I need to get my bag," she said. "Wait outside."

He looked over her head towards Rachel. "Don't start the fight again."

"Just getting my bag." She hoped she pulled off an innocent look, but Harry didn't seem convinced.

Magenta ducked away from him and trotted to the back of the shop, where she'd stowed her messenger bag. As she came back, she passed Rachel picking up sodden lingerie. She leaned in to the woman.

"You come between Harry and me again and I will drop you down a mine shaft where no one will ever find you. That's a promise."

The colour drained from Rachel's skin, but she didn't reply. With a smile, Magenta headed for Harry.

He clasped her hand in his and didn't mention that he'd seen her speak to Rachel. Together, they walked up the high street towards the house she shared with the twins. She knew she looked a sight in her sodden and ripped clothes. She didn't care. She wanted to shout from the rooftops that she wasn't stupid. Tell the world she was normal after all. She was giddy with her newfound knowledge.

In front of the grey stone wall of the old Presbyterian church, Magenta turned to Harry. Her smile was wide as she looked up at him.

"I love you, Harry Boyle."

His silver eyes grew dark as he grinned that slow, sexy grin of his.

"I knew you could say it without insulting me at the same time."

Magenta rolled her eyes. "Shut up and kiss me, you idiot."

"With pleasure." And then he did just that.

THREE MONTHS LATER

"I'm ready." Harry walked into the living room of the house he shared with Magenta.

It'd taken quite a bit of cajoling to get her to move in with him. She kept telling him that their relationship was too new, that it was too early to take such a big step. He pointed out that it couldn't be new when he'd known her since he was eight. In the end, he was pretty sure she only gave in to stop the nagging. He grinned. It was a technique he'd use again. But only for important things. Like convincing her to marry him as soon as possible.

"You're seriously going to wear that?" Magenta's voice distracted him from his self-congratulatory thoughts.

He looked down at himself. "I don't see the problem."

Magenta started laughing. "You have duct tape around your legs."

"To keep the rats out of my trousers." He wasn't stupid. He also wasn't taking any chances.

She leaned forward and sniffed. "Damn, you've sprayed yourself with pine oil, haven't you?"

Another sensible measure. He pointed to his backpack.

"I've packed some yummy rat-treat poison as well. You can never be too prepared."

Magenta eyed his pack, which was double the size of hers. "This is only a day trip, Harry—we aren't spending the night in the mine."

Thank you, Lord. Harry glanced towards heaven. He really wasn't ready for another night in the mine. He'd probably never be ready.

"Did you pack your tent too?" The sparkle of amusement in her eyes made his knees weak.

"Of course I did. The caving website said that you should be prepared for anything."

"Did the website also say that you should listen to your qualified and experienced instructor?"

"You know it did." He was so proud of her. As soon as she'd been officially diagnosed as dyslexic, she'd charged towards achieving her goals. Her self-esteem was still wobbly, but it was getting better every day. "I totally trust my guide. I know she's the best in Scotland."

She arched an eyebrow at him.

"Sorry, I meant to say in all of Europe." He smothered a grin.

Magenta gave him a regal nod. "That's much better."

She was wearing her usual black uniform, only instead of a sexy mini-dress she had on jeans and hiking boots. He still hadn't managed to get her into a blue silk dress, but he was a patient man. He had the rest of their lives to wear her down. He had managed to supplement her lingerie with a rainbow-coloured assortment of styles. It drove him crazy knowing that under her black exterior was a sexy explosion of colour that only he got to see.

He watched with growing horror as she went through his bag, discarding half the things he'd packed. Things he was *sure* he would need. He had to bite the inside of his mouth to stop from objecting. As she kept pointing out, he either trusted her to keep him safe in the mine, or he didn't. There was no middle ground. Which was a total bummer.

"Right, that's much better." She handed him the pack. "At least now you won't damage your back carting all of that around with you for the day." She eyed the clock over the mantel. "Okay, we need to go. I don't want to be late and make everyone wait."

She bounced on the spot with barely contained excitement. This was her first official tour into the mine. Part of her new business as an official guide for the local mines and caves. A business she'd called Magenta Mine. He glanced at the pile of business cards and leaflets on the table. He'd managed to talk her out of using black for her logo. Instead she'd used the colour magenta. She'd grumbled a little about pink being the wrong colour for caving, saying it was unrealistic, that caves as a whole didn't tend towards pink. He'd argued that dirt brown wouldn't be a great image either. In the end, she went for bright and attractive. Just like her.

"I can't believe I'm doing it," she told him. "Actually leading my first guided trip into the mine. I really hope people enjoy themselves."

"They will." Especially since this first tour was made up of their friends and family. Even the twins were daring to go underground. They'd bought matching pink jumpsuits for the occasion, in honour of the Magenta Mine colour scheme. Magenta had taken one look at them, shrugged in disgust and declared it was Barbie Does Caving. Matt had almost choked, he'd laughed so hard.

Harry followed Magenta to the front door, passing the framed photos she'd taken that lined the walls. His chest swelled with pride. She was an amazing photographer. She managed to make the mine seem exotic and mysterious, rather than a rat-infested hole in the ground. He shook his head. Mustn't think like that. He didn't want to lose it and run screaming from the mine. Not only would that embarrass his woman, but he'd never hear the end of it from his cousins. He wondered if there would be time to stop at the pharmacy on the way to the mine. There must be some over-the-counter anxiety medication he could buy to help him out. He reached for his mobile phone. He'd google it while they walked.

Before he could get to Google, he spotted an email from Rachel. Things were still tense between them, although the distance helped. He wouldn't be surprised if she was looking for another job. It hurt to think about it. He had eight years of friendship with her that had been damaged by her behaviour towards Magenta. He wasn't sure they'd ever get past it.

He was so busy with his phone that he didn't realise Magenta had stopped in front of him. He walked into her back. She turned on a sigh, reaching up to cup his cheek with her hand.

"You don't need medication."

Harry blinked at her. How did she know he was thinking that?

She smiled. "You were mumbling again. Don't worry. You're going to be fine in the mine. You're going to have fun."

He wasn't convinced. And he wasn't great at hiding it either. Magenta grinned at the look on his face. She pressed in until her body was flush against his. As usual, the blood in his head rushed south to enable a much more important function than allowing him to think. Magenta trailed her black-painted nails up his chest.

"You need to think about something else to take your mind off the rats." She gave him a pointed look. "Of which we won't see any, I can promise you. As soon as they hear the noise we'll be making, they'll run and hide."

He didn't bother arguing. He'd already told her every story he'd read where the rats had done the opposite.

"How about when we get home, we have a bath together and I'll wash all the dust from the tunnels off your body." She blinked up at him, a fake-innocent look in her eye that made his mouth water. He swallowed hard. "And when you're nice and clean, I'll lick you from head to toe." She leaned in and whispered, "Maybe we could tie you to the bed tonight and I can show you exactly how much fun I can have with you. Would you like that, Harry? Would you like to be at my mercy? Would you like to feel my fingers, my lips, my tongue, my hot breath, over every inch of your skin? Every. Single. Inch."

He shuddered as she gave him a wickedly mouth-watering grin. "Yeah." She nodded. "I think you'd like that a lot." She reached up, wound her fingers into his hair and pulled his head down to her. Her lips moved slowly and seductively as she tasted him. She moaned as his hand found the spot on the small of her back that drove her wild. He pulled her to him. Holding her tightly as she gasped and he took control of the kiss.

Sadly, she pushed away from him, but he was pleased to see her eyes were heavy with desire. She licked her lips, making his jeans painfully tight.

"Now, how about you think about what's going to happen *after* our excursion, rather than during it," she said.

Harry doubted he'd think about anything else. He pretended to narrow his eyes at her. "You're sneaky."

"And horny. Remember that as we walk the mine. I'm as desperate to get back here and get naked as you are." She tapped her chin in thought. "As a special treat, I'll let you know more about my plans for you throughout the day. That should keep your big brain occupied."

Damn. Now he didn't want to leave. "Maybe we could do this trip another day?"

With a laugh, Magenta tugged him out of the door and slammed it shut behind them. Guess they were still going into the mine. He let out a disappointed sigh that made her giggle.

"Thanks for wearing the present I gave you," Magenta told him as they headed for the car.

Harry looked down at the T-shirt. It was bubble-gum pink—a colour Dougal, the town's unofficial mayor, thought was a fashion statement. On the front in bold black writing were the words *Magenta Mine*. He grinned at it. He knew the shirt was supposed to advertise her business, but as far as he was concerned it told the world whom she belonged to. She was definitely his.

"You're going all caveman again, aren't you?"

He looked over his shoulder to see Magenta staring with pride at the back of his T-shirt. It said: *Property of Magenta Fraser.*

"I don't think I'm the only one," he told her. "You think you own me."

Magenta smiled knowingly, but didn't deny it was true. Harry couldn't argue otherwise. The T-shirt was right. Magenta Fraser totally owned him.

And he wouldn't have it any other way.

FIRST CHAPTER OF CALAMITY JENA

The New Jersey mob arrived in the Scottish Highlands four months after Jena Morgan. The three men strutted down Invertary high street, looking for something—or someone. Dressed like cast members of *The Sopranos*, the men fit in about as much as a shark would blend at a pool party.

Jena didn't spot them straight away. The famous go-go dancer was too busy haggling with the owner of the local hardware store.

"Please." She wasn't above pleading. Or flirting. She batted her eyelashes at the old man. He laughed. "I'm desperate and I can't afford your quote. It's going to rain and I need to patch the holes in the roof before I end up swimming around the house."

"This is Scotland, Jena, it's always going to rain. Rain does *not* constitute a desperate need." Gordon Stewart folded his arms over grey, paint-splattered overalls and grinned. The sparkle in his eye told her he was eager for her next argument. It was a dance they did every time she came into his store.

Brenda, Gordon's wife, came in from the back of the store

sipping a mug of tea. "Stop messing with the girl; give her what she needs. She's got enough on her plate sorting out the wreck she lives in without dealing with your dodgy sense of humour as well."

Brenda winked at Jena, who beamed back. Part of her wished Brenda would adopt her. If she'd had parents like the Stewarts she might have developed the ability to make smart decisions. Instead she'd grown up with a missing father and a mother obsessed with becoming the next Mariah Carey.

"Look," Jena said to Gordon. "We both know I can't afford the full price. What about a payment plan?"

He shook his head, earning an elbow in his ribs from his wife. He grunted at her before stroking his grey beard. It was his thinking pose. Jena crossed her fingers behind her back.

"Fine," he said. "How about you give me what you can afford and then work here two mornings a week to make up the difference?"

Brenda nodded her encouragement.

Jena's jaw dropped. "You can't be serious. I don't know what half this stuff is."

"I know." Gordon laughed so hard he had to wipe tears from his eyes. "It's the funniest thing I've ever seen. I read somewhere that laughing can add years to your life. Having you around will make me immortal."

"Gordon!" Brenda scowled at him. It had no effect.

Jena took a deep breath. "Okay." Like she had a choice. She pointed at him. "But you're delivering the materials for free."

"Done. You start in the morning."

"And you supply lunch."

"Only if you don't eat that rabbit crap."

"I eat anything." She couldn't afford to be fussy. "I'll see you in the morning." She pulled the heavy door open and cool October air made her skin tingle. "You evil old black-mailer," she muttered, and heard him laugh.

Waving at Brenda, Jena stepped out into the high street and was stunned anew at the picturesque quality of her new home. Streets lined with crooked whitewashed buildings, quaint little shops and a cobble-stoned road. All surrounded by emerald-green hills and reflected in a gentle blue loch. She took a deep breath and felt something settle within her. Her whole life she'd wanted a proper home, a place to belong, and she'd finally found it.

And that was when she saw them. The three men who were looking for her.

She almost fell on her backside scrambling to get back into the hardware store. "Going out the back way," she shouted, sounding more than a little hysterical.

She passed the stunned faces of the store owners as she ran straight through the shop and out the back door.

"Oh no, oh no, oh no…" She stumbled her way up the back alley in three-inch neon pink wedges, grateful she'd worn her lowest heels to town.

Her heart almost burst from her chest when she spotted her destination—the ancient grey Presbyterian church. Someone called her name. She didn't turn to see who. Instead, she picked up her pace, flying up the street on legs toned by years of dancing.

"Oh no, oh no, oh no…"

It took all her upper body strength to pull open the heavy church door.

"Coming through," she shouted at the vicar as she ran past him into the ladies' toilet.

"Jena?" His voice carried after her.

She slammed the old wooden door, bolted it and wedged a chair under the handle. Then she sank to the floor, curled her knees to her chest and rested her cheek on them. This was not happening. It was a hallucination brought on by too much DIY and not enough Pop-Tarts.

There was a thump at the door. She squealed before smacking her hands over her mouth.

"Jena, what do you think you're doing? Is this some weird American thing I don't know about?" It was the vicar, sounding grumpy—as usual.

She let out a shaky breath. Her hands fell to her knees.

"I'm claiming asylum," she shouted.

There was a pause. "You're claiming what?" the minister boomed.

Jena pulled her iPod out of her handbag, inserted her earbuds and pumped up the volume. She needed some Taylor Swift. Life was always better with Taylor.

There was more thumping. Jena closed her eyes and pretended that she hadn't seen her ex-boyfriend walking up Invertary high street.

And he definitely wasn't flanked by two goons.

With that thought, she closed her eyes and let Taylor work her magic.

* * *

Matt Donaldson, Invertary's entire police force, was already fed up with his day and he'd only been working for twenty minutes.

After dealing with yet another missing cat report, he'd been called out to the Presbyterian church. He found the ancient vicar blocking the main door, glaring up at three huge strangers. It didn't take a genius to spot that two of the men were muscle-for-hire. Although the fact one of them wore a T-shirt with the word "goon" on it helped clear things up. The third guy was obviously the boss. He looked like he'd walked straight off the set of an American mob movie. His black suit screamed custom made. The black silk shirt beneath it was open at the neck, where it flashed the obligatory gold chain. As Matt approached, Mr Suit grinned unnaturally white teeth and splayed his hands in a conciliatory gesture. The afternoon sun glinted off his pinkie ring.

Matt cocked an eyebrow at the guy, before dismissing him as he turned to the aging vicar. "What's going on?"

"The new American girl has locked herself in the toilet. She's claiming asylum." Reverend Morrison pointed to the men. "These three want to have a word with her. They were chasing her up the street when she barrelled in here."

"Frank Di Marco." The guy in the suit held out his hand. Matt didn't take it. Frank shrugged like it meant nothing. "Jena is my fiancée. We had a disagreement and she moved country. We're reconciling."

Matt didn't buy his harmless buddy routine. "Aye, I can tell by the way she's hiding in the toilet that she's eager to reconcile." He nodded to the goons. "You brought a couple of bodyguards with you to talk to your fiancée?"

Another wide smile, just as fake as the first. "These are friends of mine." He pointed at the guy wearing the goon T-shirt. "That's Joe; the big guy is Grunt."

"Grunt?" Matt looked at the big guy. He grunted. Matt nodded. That answered that.

Joe folded his arms over his joke T-shirt. His eyes betrayed an intelligence that wasn't obvious in his boss.

"So." Matt rubbed his chin. "If this is a misunderstanding, why didn't you visit Jena at her home instead of chasing her into a church? Better yet, why not call her and set up a meeting?" He hardened his eyes. "Preferably somewhere public."

A muscle ticked at the edge of Frank's jaw. "I don't have her number; she changed phones when she moved. Get her to call me, will ya? Tell her I'm real eager to see her." He put on his black sunglasses, even though the day was overcast. "Good meeting you, officer."

Frank nodded to his men, turned and sauntered back down the high street. Matt could have sworn that Joe smothered a grin as he passed.

"What the hell was that?" Matt muttered.

"Although I don't appreciate the language, I'm with you on sentiment. Looks like our newest resident is in it up to her eyeballs."

Matt allowed a small smile. "In what exactly, vicar?"

"Why, manure, boy—thick, smelly manure."

Matt let out a sigh. Jena Morgan was currently number one on the list of reasons he'd compiled for why he needed a proper police job. One far away. In a city where real crime happened. Where he wasn't called out to talk strange American women out of toilets.

"Did you ask her why she's claiming asylum? Maybe tell her that her actions aren't legal? That the church doesn't offer any more protection than she'd find in the pub?"

"Are you comparing the house of God to the local pub, son?"

Matt grinned. "I've heard better sermons in the pub."

The vicar smacked him on the back of the head. Matt rubbed it, but chuckled at the same time. "Have you talked to Jena or not?"

Reverend Morrison threw up his hands in disgust. "I tried. It's impossible. She's singing at the top of her lungs. Something about shaking herself all night long. I can't get through the door. You're going to have to deal with this."

Matt smothered a groan. "Do you have a spare key for the toilet?"

"Son, that door is about a million years old. I didn't even know it locked."

"Brilliant." He pinched the bridge of his nose. "Will it bother you if I kick it in?"

The vicar laughed. "No, but it might bother you when you break your toes. The door is several inches thick." He beamed with pride. "They don't make them like that anymore."

"Window?" Matt was quickly losing what little patience he had left.

The vicar pointed to the side of the church. "You'll know you have the right one when you hear the toneless wailing."

The vicar was right. It didn't take long to zero in on the right window. He could hear singing, or wailing, coming from inside the room. The window was level with Matt's shoulders and it wasn't locked. He peered into the darkened room, but couldn't see Jena. The ladies' toilet was the old-fashioned type, combining a room for women to wait and fix their makeup with a room for them to do their business. Matt could only see a portion of the waiting room. With a sigh, he heaved himself up and launched his body into the room.

He turned the corner and found Jena sitting on the floor beside the main door. His breath stuttered in his chest, as it usually did when he saw the woman. It was easy to under-stand why the men of Invertary were falling over themselves to date her. Unfortunately, after about ten minutes in her company, you also realised why none of those first dates led to a second—the woman was chaos personified. He'd never met anyone so easily distracted and accident-prone. She was a one-woman weapon of mass destruction.

But she was stunning. Waist-length honey-brown hair that fell in waves over golden skin. Curves, voluptuous but toned, that made a man itch to touch her. Her lips were the colour of a ripe peach and just as lush. But it was her eyes that undid him. Wide eyes the colour of warm honey. Eyes a man could melt into. He shook himself from the daze she induced.

Matt crouched down in front of Jena and tapped her knee.

Her shriek had him covering his ears.

"Stop that right now!" Matt watched as comprehension dawned in those sinful eyes. It was followed closely by relief.

"Matt." Her shoulders sagged. "I'm sorry, I thought…" She looked around nervously. "You startled me."

"Yeah, I got that from the screaming." Matt stood. "Come on, we need to get out of here." He turned towards the door.

"No." Jena scrambled to her feet. She pulled the earbuds from her ears and stuffed them into her massive canvas bag. "I claimed asylum. I'm staying here. I have water. A toilet. I can order pizza and they'll deliver through the window. I'm all set."

Matt took a deep breath and looked down at her. In her platform shoes, the top of her head made it just past his shoulders. She blinked up at him, wide-eyed and earnest. It took him a minute to figure out who she reminded him of, and then it hit him—the cat from Shrek. He closed his eyes for a second to regroup.

"Number one." Matt held up a finger. "This is Invertary. There is no pizza delivery. Number two. You can't claim asylum. There's no such thing."

"Of course there is. I saw it on TV."

"Those are political asylum seekers. Generally they register with the government, who then reviews their case. They live in houses the councils provide. They don't hole up in church toilets."

She seemed confused. The cutest little lines appeared between her brows. "I didn't see that show. I was talking about the movies. Clint Eastwood. That sort of thing."

He stared at her as his brain rebooted. "You mean cowboy movies. Westerns?"

She smiled widely. "Exactly. But if you need me to register, hand the paperwork through the window and I'll sign it."

For a minute he was tempted to give up on the conversation and leave her in the bathroom. "Jena, those movies aren't real. They're fiction."

"Those movies are based on historical fact. They have to research them and stuff."

"They're also based in America. You're in Scotland. Even if they were real, we don't let you claim asylum in churches over here. Come on, it's time to leave. The Weight Watchers group meet in half an hour and they like to use the toilet before the weigh-in. They won't be happy to find the door locked."

She eyed him suspiciously. "How would you know something like that?"

"I have a mother and two younger sisters. I know everything there is to know about needless weight loss and insane diets. Now, let's get out of here."

She grabbed his arm. "I can't leave. I..." She looked around, maybe hoping that an excuse would present itself. At last her shoulders slumped and she seemed resigned. "There's someone in town looking for me and I need to hide. Or run." A thought occurred to her. Her eyes went wide. "Wait a minute. Are you going to arrest me? Did he send you in here to take me to the big house?" Her brow scrunched. "No, that can't be it. He wouldn't send in the cops." Her face went white. "Those have to be Rizzoni's men he's got with him. There can only be one reason he brought mob lackeys to Scotland." She took a deep breath. "He's going to kill me. I claim asylum."

With a screech, she ran into a toilet stall and locked the door.

* * *

Jena slammed the toilet lid down and sat on it. She was going to die. She knew it. Why else would Frank come all the way to Scotland? It wasn't as though he loved to travel. He thought New York was too far to visit, and that was only a two-hour drive from Atlantic City.

"Jena." Matt sounded like he was gritting his teeth.

Jena felt instantly guilty. It wasn't his fault she'd brought all this trouble to town. He was doing the best he could, but a small-town cop in the Scottish Highlands wasn't equipped to deal with the Atlantic City mob.

"Tell me what's going on right now." His commanding tone sent shivers down her spine. Still, she didn't answer.

"Jena? Why did you think I was going to arrest you? Why do you think Frank wants to kill you?"

Jena chewed down on her thumbnail before stopping when she remembered she would never be able to afford another manicure.

Matt sucked in an irritated breath. "I'm ten seconds away from ripping that door off its hinges, dragging you to the station and putting you and Frank Di Marco in a room until someone tells me what's going on."

Nausea assaulted her at his words. At least she was in the right place if she wanted to vomit.

"Jena. Talk. Now. Why do you think your fiancé is going to harm you?"

She sat up straight. "Fiancé? What fiancé?"

He let out an exasperated sigh. "Frank Di Marco."

Jena shot to her feet and pointed at the door. "He is not my fiancé. He's a cheating man-whore, that's what he is. He's never even proposed. Not that I would have accepted. But there has to be a proposal for there to be a fiancé."

"Okay, so he isn't your fiancé. Why would he say he is?"

"Insanity?" She was pretty sure that was the underlying reason for everything Frank did.

"Tell me what's going on or I can't help you." A vision of Officer Donaldson's deep blue eyes looking all earnest and stern flashed in her mind. She wavered.

"Can you have him kicked out of town? Maybe deported?" She tried not to sound too hopeful.

"Possibly. If I know the truth."

Jena bit her bottom lip as she shuffled foot to foot.

"It will be okay." The cop's soothing brogue almost undid her. "Tell me what the problem is. Trust me, Jena."

Jena felt herself cave. She took a shaky breath, grateful she was telling her stupid story from behind a door where she couldn't see the judgment in his eyes. "Frank and I lived together for a while. He cheated on me with a series of strippers. I'm pretty sure they were all called Candy." She couldn't keep the snide tone out of her words, which made her feel ashamed. She was better than that. She was better than Frank Di Marco. "Anyway, when I found out about the strippers, I lost the plot a little. I kicked Frank out of the house, sold everything we owned and used the money to move here."

She took a deep breath while waiting for his reaction.

"Okay, so far I'm not hearing anything that has me worried. I don't see why the man would come all this way to get revenge over you selling his stuff."

She bit her bottom lip. "I also sold his perfectly restored 1966 Chevrolet Chevelle. He loved that car more than anything. Definitely more than me."

There was a pause. "You sold the man's classic car?"

Jena frowned at the door. "Should I have hit it with a baseball bat and set fire to the seats instead?"

"Point made. Carry on."

Jena rolled her eyes. Men and their cars. "That's all there is to tell. Once everything was gone, I surfed the net looking for a new place to live. I remembered my mom talking about Invertary—she's a huge Josh McInnes fan and gives me updates on what he's doing. Next thing I knew, I was looking at the town website. Then the town's real estate site. After drowning my sorrow in a bottle of tequila, I bought a house." She paused. "And here I am."

There was silence for a minute. If it wasn't for the sound of his breathing, she would have thought he'd left her.

"Let me get this right. You sold everything the guy owned, without his knowledge, and bought a house in Scotland with the proceeds?"

She felt her cheeks burn. "I had a holiday in Paris too. But bear in mind that he isn't really a guy. He's a scum-sucking man-whore."

For a moment she heard nothing, and then deep laughter echoed throughout the room.

"Remind me never to piss you off," the cop said between gasps.

Jena frowned at the closed door, wondering what the correct response was to that statement.

"Am I going to be arrested for selling his stuff?" It had been worrying her.

"You didn't do it in Scotland, Jena."

"Will they extradite me?"

The cop started laughing again. "I only talked to Frank for a couple of minutes, but I figure the cops in Atlantic City will give you a standing ovation rather than charge you with theft. I don't know much about American law, but in Scotland if you live with someone for a couple of years you're considered to be in a common-law marriage and your property is shared. Over here the stuff you sold would have legally belonged to you too."

"I did put a lot of money into our relationship. I kept us afloat for years while Frank tried to make it big."

"Well, there you go, then. Can you come out of the toilet now?"

"I can't leave here, Matt. Frank must be here for revenge. He'll want his money back. Along with his car. And I don't have either."

"Come out of the toilet, Jena. I'll deal with Frank."

She cracked the door open and peered up at him. Instead of the usual disapproval, his eyes were sparkling with amusement. It wasn't an improvement.

"Let's get you home," he said.

She shook her head. "He has to know where I live. I can't go back there."

"Are you afraid he'll hurt you?" His features turned to stone. "Has he ever hurt you?"

"No." He didn't look convinced. "No, he's never lifted his hand to me."

"Then why are you afraid? Why not just talk to the man?"

"Didn't you hear me in there?" She gestured to the toilet stall where she'd spilled her guts to him. "He's here with Vince Rizzoni's boys."

Matt held up his hands in exasperation. "So?"

"They're the mob. Frank got into bed with the guy about a year ago—along with every other skanky woman in stilettos on the East Coast."

His huge hands clasped her shoulders. "Focus, Jena."

For a few seconds she was too mesmerised by his perfectly squared jaw and deep-set eyes to focus on anything other than the man in front of her.

"You were telling me about Frank and the mob," he prompted.

Jena felt herself blush. "Yeah, he started hanging with Vince's men. He changed. Became harder, more cagey. He kept secrets, other than the women. I didn't like the men who started to visit. Some of them scared me."

"Those guys here today, were they the ones visiting?"

She shook her head. "Other guys. Rougher. I felt like I didn't know Frank anymore. I was worried and he wouldn't listen to me. He'd get angry. Real angry. I would like to think he isn't capable of harming me, but he changed, and I don't know for sure what he's capable of now."

Matt let out a heavy sigh. "Okay. There's no need to worry. You aren't in America anymore. The mob doesn't have a lot of pull here. I'll deal with Frank and find out what he wants."

"I think it's best if I stay here until you have a chat with him."

"You can't hide in here."

Jena disagreed. She wasn't proud. She could definitely hide. Hiding was exactly what she needed to do. She took a step back into the toilet stall and slammed the door shut.

"Thank you for helping me. I really appreciate it, and I hate being rude like this, but I think it's best if I stay here until you sort out Frank."

"Jena." Matt's tone was a threat.

Jena swallowed hard as she put her earbuds back in place. She'd do something nice for the cop later as a thank you. Something that didn't involve money, as she had none. She'd bake him cookies but she couldn't cook. Maybe she'd teach him to dance? Everybody could use some dancing skills. Yeah, that was a great idea.

She sat on the toilet lid, tuned out Matt's shouting and let Taylor Swift's voice calm her racing heart.

ABOUT THE AUTHOR

I'm a Scot, living in New Zealand and married to a Dutch man. I write contemporary romance with a humorous bent – this is mainly due to the fact I have an odd sense of humour and can't keep it out of anything I do! If I wasn't a writer, I'd like to be Buffy the Vampire Slayer, or Indiana Jones. Unfortunately, both these roles have already been filled. Which may be a good thing as I have no fighting skills, wouldn't know a precious relic if it hit me in the face and have an aversion to blood. When I'm not living in my head, I'm a mother to two kids, several pet sheep, one dog, four cats, three alpacas, two miniature horses, eight guinea pigs and an escape artist chicken.